SCRATCH PAD

The fourth book in
the NOTED! series

Kathy J. Jacobson

D1292426

LITTLE CREEK PRESS®
AND BOOK DESIGN

Mineral Point, Wisconsin USA

Little Creek Press®
A Division of Kristin Mitchell Design, Inc.
5341 Sunny Ridge Road
Mineral Point, Wisconsin 53565

Book Design and Project Coordination:
Little Creek Press

Second Edition
February 2017

Printed in Wisconsin, United States of America

For more information or to order books:
kjjacobsonauthor@gmail.com
or visit www.littlecreekpress.com

Library of Congress Control Number: 2016959824

ISBN-10: 1-942586-21-3
ISBN-13: 978-1-942586-21-0

Dedication

For all parents of "angels"

Chapter One

John sat at the table in the breakfast nook, scratching his head as he gazed at the end-of-the-month report glowing from his laptop screen. He glanced at his approaching wife and moved over so she could sit down next to him.

"Who would give one million dollars to the Esperanza Workshop, Jillian?" he asked, referring to the non-profit acting studio they had christened on March the twenty-seventh, their "gift" to themselves on their first anniversary.

Jillian slid into the seat, putting her arm around his shoulders and her head next to his as she scanned the report.

"Your guess is as good as mine, sweetheart. It's obvious the person doesn't want us—or anyone—to know. I just thank God for whomever it was."

"Me, too. I never would have believed we could be doing so well at the end of our first month of operation. And one of the best things is that generous donations like this one snowball into other generous donations. Look at all of them! They aren't all a *million dollars,* but they are far more than I would have ever dreamed of in a *million years*. It's truly amazing," John said, closing the laptop and turning to his wife, his eyes bright with happiness.

"Almost as amazing as you," Jillian replied, and kissed him.

"Do we really have to go?" he asked softly when the kiss ended.

"Let's see—you're the lead male actor, and I'm one of the screenwriters and assistant directors/consultants. I think Carson would appreciate our presence at the production meeting," she said, reluctantly sliding back out of the seat. She stood up, her hand still on John's shoulder.

"I wonder if Carson got the female lead he was so excited about. He's been so hush-hush on this one," John said, curiosity in his voice.

"It sounded like he was hoping to have her signed in time for today's meeting. I wonder who she will be this time?" Jillian asked, a far-off look on her face. She wanted to tack on, "*it couldn't be any worse than Monica Morgan,*" but she held her tongue. Monica, John's former girlfriend and co-star on the medical drama, *O.R.,* had made John's last movie project sheer misery—for both of them. Monica had relentlessly pursued John from day one. Things had only taken a positive turn after Jillian had flown to Alaska, where the actors were filming on location. Not only had Jillian made her presence known, but she had spoken honestly with Monica about the situation.

In a surprising turn of events, Monica not only stopped hounding John, but actually apologized to him for her poor behavior— during the movie and in their past relationship—helping to heal wounds that had been festering for years. By the end of the shoot, Monica was like a different person, even giving up her seat on the airplane back to Los Angeles so Jillian and John could fly home together. It had been a miraculous "one-eighty," to say the least. Jillian shook her head in disbelief as she recalled that final event, the last time both she and John had seen Monica.

John stood and faced Jillian. He saw her expression and recognized the look. "Whomever it is, Jillian, you have nothing to worry about," he replied, and hugged her close.

"I know." Jillian really didn't worry about John. She had complete trust in him. But she knew from recent experience that she couldn't always say that about some of the people with whom he worked. She would just have to trust that Carson Stone wouldn't put her in a position like he had the last time with Monica. It couldn't get much worse than that—*or could it?*

It was only the second time Jillian had been in Carson Stone's office, which occupied three-quarters of the top floor of a building not far from the studio. The views from the three ceiling-to-floor "walls of windows" stunned Jillian even more this time than on her previous visit. Carson sat back in his chair behind his glass desk. The entire room made the world feel somehow transparent.

It was in this office that Carson had made John and Jillian an offer they could not refuse—to work together on his latest project, a suspenseful drama set in the medical world. That was why Carson wanted Jillian to be part of the project. Her twenty-five years of nursing experience had been invaluable in Alaska, as she saved the day when the actor Chase Cheekwood dislocated his finger during a fight scene, far from a hospital or clinic. Not only did she help Chase medically, but she gave suggestions to Carson and his assistant director that they actually ended up using in the film.

After finding out that Jillian was the author of a book and had legitimate writing skills, along with her medical background, Carson asked her to work with a talented new screenwriter to help him make the script more credible. Jillian felt quite undeserving of this honor and hoped that she would not disappoint Carson in the end.

Jillian and the young screenwriter, Nolan, were in the process of informing Carson and the others about the adjustments they had made to the script when Carson's intercom buzzed. He pushed a button and spoke. "Yes?"

A voice on the other end responded, "Your guest has arrived, Mr. Stone."

"Send her in," he said, an excited look growing on his face.

Jillian surmised, correctly, that the "guest" was the female lead for the movie. There was a knock on the door, and a woman opened the door into the room. She turned to someone in the doorway and gestured for her to come in. Carson stood up, as did the five others in the room.

Carson walked over to the woman and extended his hand to hers, shaking it gently. He then turned to the group. "Everyone, I would like you to meet our Dr. Serena Torres. Please welcome—Luz."

The group was silent for a moment. The woman's presence seemed to fill the entire room. Jillian suddenly wondered if Carson Stone was purposely trying to drive her insane. She watched as Luz glided across the room toward them, dressed in a bright red dress that flattered her shapely form—although Luz most likely would look great in a flour sack, Jillian thought.

Luz. Jillian didn't know if Luz had any other name. She probably didn't need one. Luz was the "Marilyn Monroe" of South America, a Peruvian beauty who had made countless movies and the front page of even more magazines.

The word "*luz*" means "light" in Spanish. Its secondary meaning is "power" or "electricity." Luz perfectly fit all of these descriptions, as she flashed an electric smile, extending her smooth, bronze, beautiful arm and hand toward the others in the room as introductions ensued. Jillian thought poor Nolan might faint for a moment. She didn't even glance John's way, trying to avoid his perceptive eyes, or worse yet, witness a look similar to what the other males in the room were giving the stunning figure before them.

Luz took Jillian's hand and shook it. Jillian, who finally had her hands looking and feeling decent by her standards, felt like she had long ago when a hand cream vendor had called her out in a shopping mall, noticing her dry, red, and rough abused hands—the hands of a nurse and mother. She felt self-conscious for an instant as she touched Luz' perfect skin.

Jillian decided she would just have to grin and bear the situation, so she looked Luz straight in the eyes, smiled, and shook her hand firmly. Luz' eyes reminded her of the countertop in her and John's honeymoon house on the ocean. They were black and shiny, like they had just been polished. Yet as Jillian looked deeply into them, there was something else. She couldn't quite put her finger on it, but it seemed like some sort of sadness or unhappiness. Jillian always had an uncanny way of reading that type of thing in people—almost like a sixth sense.

"Let's sit down," Carson said. He showed Luz to a comfortable seat in the circle they had created with a soft gray leather couch and a number of chairs.

Jillian wasn't sure, but she thought that Carson seemed a bit nervous. She had never seen this powerful director anything close to that before, but it wasn't every day that someone was in the presence of such a natural physical beauty—someone who was not only a top "cover girl" but possessed genuine acting skills as well. Jillian had always enjoyed Luz' work on the screen, although she sometimes wished the woman would be cast in a more serious role. Well, now that "serious role" was finally a reality for Luz. The only drawback, from Jillian's viewpoint, was that Luz was working opposite *her* husband.

Jillian knew the script. There was a fair amount of kissing as well as a bedroom scene. Like the bedroom scene from John's previous movie, it was not very long, and it had also recently been rewritten. Jillian had felt strange suggesting that she and Nolan tweak the scene. She didn't want to appear to be controlling it because of her connection to John. But at the same time, she didn't want it to become the focus of the movie or be vulgar in any way. She and Nolan had come to a reasonable and tasteful compromise, she believed. Now, looking at Luz, Jillian thought that maybe she should have pushed harder to make it even tamer.

She snapped back to reality as Carson mentioned her name. "I'm sorry, would you repeat what you just said, Carson?" she asked with a hint of embarrassment.

"I was just telling Luz about your medical background and what a help you were on our last film, even when you weren't on the payroll," he said, smiling. Carson seemed like he was trying to be extra nice to her and looked a bit apologetic as he spoke.

The meeting went on for another hour, but Jillian felt like she heard nothing during that time. She wondered if she had said anything that made any sense at all during the few times she actually spoke.

Mostly it was Carson and the producer doing the speaking, with the rest of them listening. They would have a read-through of the script next week, now that Luz was on board. Then the week after that, they were going to begin filming. Luckily, this time they wouldn't have to travel out of the state, as the locations were all in California. Given, it is a large state, but it was nothing like the trek to Alaska, complete with small airplanes flying into blizzards!

The producer and Carson wanted Luz to stay a bit longer to talk. The rest of them were dismissed and headed to the elevator. Nolan and the assistant director got off a few floors down, where they each had offices, although Nolan's was only temporary. Jillian had been offered a temporary one as well, but had declined, preferring to do her work at home.

When the elevator doors closed, John took Jillian's hand in his and squeezed it. She could tell he wanted to say something, but they were going to be down on the ground floor in just a few moments, and it wasn't the best time to begin a conversation. Or perhaps, she thought, he was at a loss for the appropriate words to say.

The elevator doors opened. John sometimes released her hand in a public setting, but he held it all the way to the Land Rover. He opened the door for her, and she got in. He went around to his door and hopped into the vehicle.

"Have I told you today how much I love you, Mrs. Romano?" he asked, turning toward her.

She smiled at him. "I think maybe you did, but I could stand to hear it again right now," she said honestly.

"Jillian, I love you today. I will love you tomorrow. And I will love you forever. How's that?" he asked, with that grin that melted her heart.

"That's a good start," she said.

"Then, how about this?" he added, then pulled her into a huge kiss. Rarely did John kiss her anywhere that someone could take a photo of them, but he apparently didn't care at that moment. He wanted to make a point—and the point was well-taken.

Two thousand miles away from John and Jillian, Tommy Romano sat at his desk in his office on Chicago's north side. He held a framed photograph in his hands. Tommy gazed wistfully at a photo of his family, taken during a family vacation two years before in the Florida Keys. Everyone smiled as they stood on the sunny, white sand beach, the blue-green ocean and white surf serving as their backdrop.

He couldn't believe how much his son, John Anthony, had changed in such a short time. He was three inches taller at present, and since working out with the Northwestern football team, he was also about thirty pounds heavier—all muscle. In the photo he looked like a teenager. Now he looked like a man, and he stood two inches taller than his father and his great-uncle, John.

Tommy's daughter, Alison, looked like a child to him in the photo. She wasn't really, but compared to the almost sixteen-year-old she was now, soon old enough to test for her driver's license, she looked like a baby. Where had the time, and his little girl, gone?

And Maria. She was in her bikini, with a figure like that of a college-aged woman, rather than a mother of two teenagers. Her brown hair was blowing in the breeze, and her smile was wide. Tommy's arm was around her waist, and he was half-looking at the camera, half-looking at Maria. He noticed the look on his face—it was one he hadn't seen in a while. He rubbed his finger gently over the image of his wife until he was startled by a knock on the office door.

"Come in," he said, putting the photograph back into its place on his desk. He looked up to see who it was, and smiled a classic Romano smile.

"Romano," his boss said, sticking his head into the door of the office. "I'd like you to meet our new associate."

Tommy stood up from his desk and buttoned his suit jacket. His boss of the last fifteen years entered the room, then stepped aside so the person behind him could enter as well.

Tommy hoped that he didn't look the way he felt—stunned. Standing in front of him was one of the most beautiful women he had ever seen in person. She had long, thick hair, with a wave to it and streaks of different shades of blonde, which appeared to be natural. Her eyes were a bright, sparkling sky blue, and her complexion was what his wife would have described as "peaches and cream." Maria often lamented her olive-colored skin, and like many people, wished she had features other than her own.

The woman extended her hand to him, and he shook it. There was an air of confidence about her as she introduced herself. "Amanda Richards," she said.

"Thomas Romano," he answered, using the name he used in the business world.

"Yes, I've heard about you," she said, staring him straight in the eyes.

Her stare made Tommy a bit uncomfortable and self-conscious, so he looked away.

"Well, don't believe everything you hear," he replied.

"Ms. Richards comes to us from the Boston office," his boss mentioned. "Maybe the three of us could have lunch together. Right now, I'm having Amanda meet as many people on the staff as possible before our board meeting tomorrow."

Tommy looked at the calendar on his phone to make sure that he had nothing scheduled. "I think that will work," he said.

"We will meet you downstairs in the lobby at noon," his boss said, and then he and Ms. Richards began to leave. Amanda turned and smiled at Tommy as she left, giving him another deep look.

The door to the office closed, and he sat back down in his chair. He stared at the door for a moment, then his eyes drifted back to the photo of his family. He wished he was back on that beach with his wife and kids again, back to a day when they actually had time for vacations.

Since Maria had begun her business, they barely had time for a few hours together, let alone weekends or holidays, and certainly not for vacations. Their only venture in the past year had been a long weekend to California to attend the surprise anniversary celebration for John and Jillian the month before. Even when they were home, it was different. John Anthony lived in a dorm on campus, and Alison was always busy with something at school or doing homework with her friends. They were going to go on a college tour with her in late June, but that just wasn't the same as a week at the beach with all of them together.

With a deep sigh, Tommy swiveled his chair around and stared out the office window, a faraway look in his eyes.

"Unbelievable," Jillian said as they pulled up to the gate of their property and saw that no one was waiting outside of it with a camera. "How did we make it to and from our house, and even steal a kiss in the car at the studio, and not have one person snap our photo?"

"I don't know," John answered. "There must be something or someone else who's gathering their attention today. It must be something big. Won't they be surprised when they find out they missed Carson Stone introducing Luz as his lead female for the movie? I can't believe he got her in there without anyone noticing."

They pulled through the gate, and it closed behind them. They didn't even notice the old, silver Buick parked down the block on the other side of the street. They were too engrossed in their conversation. The driver watched as their car disappeared through the iron gates.

When they got into the house, Jillian looked at her phone to see if she had any text messages and noticed what was trending on the Internet.

"Oh, no," she said.

"What's wrong, sweetheart?" John asked.

"I think I have the answer about the paparazzi."

John peered over her shoulder. "Who is the poor lout this time?" he asked.

Jillian lifted up her phone. "Monica," she said. "Her son ran someone over while driving drunk."

"Oh, no, is right," he said.

They hadn't heard much from Monica since filming had wrapped for John's previous movie. She and her husband, Ben Bastien, along with their twin twenty-three-year-old sons, had gone to their favorite resort together a week after the filming ended. They had done a lot of talking and healing, and even had some fun together for the first time in years. Monica had briefly texted Jillian, thanking her again for encouraging her to reach out to her estranged family and mentioning that they were doing much better. Jillian hadn't heard from her in a couple of weeks now, figuring no news was good news, but now this.

"Poor Monica," Jillian said seriously. "I'll have to let her know that she can call me if she wants someone to talk to, or ask if there is any way I can be of help." One of Jillian's nightly prayers was that God would help her be a helper to someone each new day.

John turned her gently toward himself. "Jillian Johnson Romano, you are the only person I know who would even think of making an offer like that to a person who has made your life so miserable in the past. That's one of the reasons I love you so much," he said, stroking her hair.

"Actually, I think you know another person who would, too," Jillian said.

"Really? Who?" John asked sincerely.

"You. You would help Monica if she asked, wouldn't you?"

"Of course," he said.

"See. And that, John D. Romano, is one of the reasons I love *you* so much," she said, and kissed him.

Chapter Two

Marty simply stared at her mother when Jillian revealed the name of John's new co-star. They were on a video chat again, as Marty was nearing the end of her special semester at Stanford Medical School, and there was no time for family visits at present. Besides, the two of them were pretty comfortable with the arrangement, as it had been their only form of communication for almost two years when Marty had been an intern in Senegal.

Finally Marty spoke. "Luz. *The* Luz?"

"Uh-huh," Jillian said, nodding her head affirmatively.

"Wow," Marty marveled.

"Yes, that would be an appropriate response to the situation—and the person," Jillian said.

"What did Dad say when he found out?" Marty asked.

"He told me how much he loves me—today, tomorrow, and always—and that I have nothing to be worried about," Jillian relayed.

"Of course you don't. Dad is crazy about you, Mom. But *Luz*—wow!"

"You already said that, Marty, and that's not really helping," Jillian replied.

"Sorry, Mama," Marty said. "But you know Dad's not lying. And if any marriage can make it through this, I know that yours can. You two are like a living advertisement for marriage, you know."

"Thanks, honey. I know you're right. I just wish there didn't have to be so many challenges every step of the way, but I guess that's life," Jillian said. "Speaking of challenges, any news on your next step? And how about Michael?"

"We have applied to a number of residency programs, all but two of them in Africa. I just hope we don't end up on opposite ends of the continent," she said. Marty and Michael were both students in global health, Michael at Stanford, and Marty at Harvard. They met while working together in Senegal and had fallen in love. Marty had been ecstatic when she had been offered a special project semester at Stanford at the last minute, or else the two would have been three thousand miles apart instead of living down the hall from one another in student housing.

"I'll let you know the minute I hear anything. It shouldn't be too long now," Marty added excitedly. The residency would be the last leg of her schooling before she became a full-fledged doctor.

The two said goodbye, and Jillian pushed her contact number for Carol. It wouldn't be long until Carol would retire from her position with the University of Wisconsin School of Nursing. There was going to be a celebration honoring her, and Jillian was working hard to find a way to be there and surprise her. She would talk to Carson Stone about it soon. In Jillian's mind, he "owed" her after casting Luz as John's co-star.

"Hi, Carol," Jillian said into the phone.

"Hi yourself," Carol answered in an unusual tone of voice.

"You sound...I'm not sure how you sound," Jillian said honestly.

"That's not surprising, because I'm not sure how I feel. One moment I am so excited. I cannot wait to be with Jerry, to live together like an actual married couple. I love him and miss him so much it physically hurts. But on the other hand, I'm trying to pack up my house, I'm starting to box up some things in my office, and I'm trying not to cry every time someone else says how much they will miss me. This has been my life for so long."

"It's understandable that you should feel all those different feelings, Carol," Jillian said to her long-time mentor and friend. "There are so many good things going on, and there are so many difficult ones, too. I'm praying for you—I feel your pain."

"I know you do, Jillian, and speaking of that, I sense a bit of it in your voice, too," Carol responded. Carol and Marty could always tell things about Jillian just by the sound of her voice, and vice versa, as they shared such deep and special relationships.

"Oh, it's nothing compared to the things you are experiencing," Jillian said, trying not to dwell on the movie.

"But if it is causing you pain of some sort, it is best to talk about it, even if it seems *minor*. You don't want it to turn into something *major*," her wise friend suggested.

"You are right," Jillian said with a slight sigh.

Jillian proceeded to tell Carol the saga revolving around the casting of Luz.

"I just didn't think it could be any worse than Monica Morgan," she said. "I guess I was wrong."

"I don't know about that. Give this woman a chance, Jillian. She might not be the person everyone thinks she is. And don't forget what you *do* know—that you are married to a man who absolutely cherishes you. There aren't too many relationships out there like the one you and John share, and Jerry and I now have, too," Carol said, a bit of happiness returning to her voice. "If anyone's relationship can endure this situation, it's yours. Don't forget that."

Jillian had already heard a similar reminder from her daughter and was beginning to feel better about everything as they said their goodbyes. Soon she would hopefully surprise Carol in

Madison, then they would be welcoming her to Los Angeles on a permanent basis.

Carol and Jerry had purchased an adorable bungalow in a neighborhood that was just starting to regain popularity. John and Jillian had given Jerry a good price for his home in Stanford, and not having to pay a real estate commission helped him secure a good down payment on the home in Los Angeles. The house was located between John and Jillian's neighborhood and Alan and Bev's neighborhood. Alan was John's agent, and Bev was Jerry's sister, so it was a perfect situation for everyone.

Jillian smiled as she turned to her laptop. She was just going to begin the next chapter in her new book about pregnancy and infant losses when her phone flashed an incoming call. It was Monica Morgan.

At first Jillian thought Monica must have dialed her number accidentally. There didn't appear to be anyone on the other end of the line when she said hello. But just when she was going to hang up, she heard something—like a stifled sob.

"Monica—is that you?" Jillian asked, concerned.

"Yessss, it's me," she answered in a soft and sorrowful voice.

"Tell me what is happening, Monica, so I can help you," Jillian said in her old nurse's voice. She knew what the Internet was saying, but she didn't want to presume to know the truth of the matter.

"Nobody can help this time. It's...my son...Brent," she said, and began crying again.

"Monica, take some deep breaths. You can do this," Jillian assured her. "What happened to Brent?"

"It didn't happen to him. He...he...was drinking...and driving... and he hit someone. It was a girl, Jillian, just a bit younger than he is. She might die, Jillian, and if that happens..." Monica began to cry harder again.

"Where are you now?" Jillian asked. "Is there someone with you?"

"I'm at the police station," she said. "Ben is in Southeast Asia filming a new movie, and I can't reach him. Bart is in play rehearsal for a role he just got—he was so excited—and now this. He and his brother are so close—they can almost read each other's minds. He's going to be so upset..."

"Monica, would you like me to come and be with you?" Jillian found herself asking.

"You...you would do that?" she asked incredulously.

"Of course. What's the address?"

She heard Monica ask someone for the address, then she relayed it to Jillian.

Jillian closed her laptop. She texted John quickly as to her plan, grabbed her keys, and was off.

Jillian had to admit that the police station on North Rexford Drive in Beverly Hills was one of the nicest-looking law enforcement facilities she had ever seen. She had planned to park in front of the building, but when she noticed the news vans and the mass of reporters and cameras surrounding the door, she moved on.

She drove down a block to park, put on her sunglasses, and walked slowly toward the building. There was an officer heading toward a side entrance, and Jillian followed her. When some of the reporters tried to follow them, the woman told them to back off, that there were real people with real things to do working today, or needing help, and to please stay out of the way. For whatever reason, they actually listened to the woman, who Jillian later learned was a sergeant on the Beverly Hills force.

Kathy J. Jacobson

The woman turned to Jillian. "I'm counting on it that you are not one of them, am I correct?" she inquired as she opened the door.

"I promise, I'm not. I'm here to support a friend whose son was arrested this afternoon," she said.

"Monica Morgan?" she asked.

"Yes," Jillian replied.

"Good. She's going to need it," the sergeant said matter-of-factly, then disappeared down the hallway toward a private office door.

That didn't sound very encouraging to Jillian, as she looked around for Monica. She was gazing about when a gentleman in a suit asked if he could be of help. He introduced himself as a detective and told her he would tell Ms. Morgan that she was there. Jillian watched as he went down another short hallway and then motioned to her to proceed. He opened the door into a small room, where Monica sat at a square metal table, her eyes swollen and red from crying.

Jillian took a seat next to her and put her hand on Monica's shoulder.

"I am so sorry, Monica," she said softly.

Monica kept staring ahead, but finally spoke. "I thought things were finally getting better for us," she said in a quivering voice.

Jillian just sat and waited for her to continue. "Ben finally called. He's starting his trip home tomorrow, but won't get here until the next day. He's beside himself. And Bart—I don't know what to say to him. This is going to kill him," she said, "especially if that young woman dies..."

"Let's pray she doesn't," Jillian replied.

"*You* can do that," Monica told her, somewhat sharply. "I don't pray."

Jillian thought about saying that it might be a good time to start, but held her tongue. She just said a silent prayer for Monica and her family, and especially for the young woman who was injured and fighting for her life, and her family.

"What's happening with Brent?" Jillian asked.

"They won't let anyone see him except his lawyer—not even me," she said. "Our lawyer is with him now. There will be an arraignment Monday morning, then he will be charged. This is his third offense, Jillian. Even if the girl survives, he is going to be in big trouble. We've tried to get him help, but he keeps saying that he doesn't have a problem—he just has bad luck—but I know he's lying. We don't know how to help him."

Jillian knew enough about addictions to understand that if Brent didn't accept the fact that he had a problem, he would be unlikely to overcome it. "I'll pray for him, too," Jillian said quietly.

Monica nodded her head and began to softly sob. Jillian put her arm around Monica's shoulders again and let her cry.

John was making a salad when Jillian walked into the kitchen hours later. She wearily set her purse down, took off her shoes, and walked over to the counter where he was wiping his hands on a towel and turning toward her.

He extended his arms to her, and she fell into them, putting her head on his chest. He kissed the top of her head and rubbed her back.

"How did it go?" he asked.

"It's not good. They won't even let Monica see her son. Ben won't be back until the day after tomorrow, and she has to tell her other son about his brother now. I dropped her off at the theater. He was in a rehearsal for a show he is so excited about. Monica is so sad. Everything seemed to be looking up, and then this. And it could get worse if the young woman dies."

"You're right, it's not good," he said.

She lifted her head and looked at John. "It sounds like Brent has a real problem, and he just won't, or can't, come to terms with it."

"I know how that can feel, especially when you're young. You are so sure you can beat it by yourself, or that it's not really a problem," he said. "It's a hard thing to admit."

"How did you do it?" she asked.

"Well, as much as my brother drove me crazy, I have him to thank in some ways. He made some comment about it, and that was enough impetus to make me determined to prove him wrong. And then there was Tommy. He looked up to me so much—I just couldn't let him down. I would have died for that kid, so I started going to meetings, saw a doctor and a counselor, and got on track. About that same time, everything seemed to take off in my career, so it was pretty easy to do for a long time. But it came back to me again—after O.R. and some of my personal disappointments— and then I had to begin the process all over again. It's been so many years now, thank God."

"Yes, thank God," she said and hugged him. "I'm feeling very fortunate tonight." In her mind, she was thinking about the amazingly easy time she had had raising her daughter. She was also thinking about John, and how he had kept his painkiller addiction in check for twenty-one years now. It was hard to even imagine how it must have been back then, and she was secretly happy she didn't know. She also felt hopeful, too, that if John could go into and stay in recovery for so long, that Brent could, too.

"Me, too," John said, then hugged her again.

Chapter Three

As Jillian threw a load of laundry into the dryer the next morning, she thought about how parenting was not for the faint of heart. Even though Marty had been an easy child to raise, there were still moments of challenge and heartache, including the horrific scare when she thought Marty might have contracted Ebola. The thought made her shiver as she closed the dryer door. She hit the start button, and her cell went off simultaneously.

It was her good friend, Karen. She was hoping that perhaps she was calling with news of the adoption date for their foster son, Ricardo, who liked to be called "Rick." Rick had been recently orphaned, his abusive father dying just months before. But instead, she found herself listening to another mother who was in "panic mode."

"We can't find Rick!" Karen screamed into the phone.

"Slow down," Jillian said softly, trying not to panic herself. The boy, whom John and Jillian had met even before Karen and Robert had, had come to mean a lot to both of them.

"What happened, Karen?"

"Robert took the day off today. We all had breakfast together, then the plan was to do some gardening and other chores in the yard. We told Rick we needed to do that before he and Robert could play catch. He seemed okay with that, and he had gone upstairs to get his baseball and glove for later. Robert and I went to the yard, and we thought he would be right out. When he didn't appear, Robert went in to see if everything was okay, and he was gone! Maybe he didn't like the idea of doing the chores—we don't know. There was a broken vase below the fireplace mantel, his glove and ball were on the floor, but he was nowhere to be found. We looked all over the house and the street, and no one seems to have seen him. Robert is on his cell phone calling the police. Jillian, if anything happens to him, I'll..." Karen didn't finish her sentence, but started crying instead.

"I'll be right there," she said. John was downtown at the Esperanza Workshop meeting with a group of young actors. He rarely had an opportunity to do that, so Jillian decided she would not call him until the acting classes were done at noon.

Jillian's heart was pounding as she drove toward Karen's. She was remembering the time that she lost sight of Marty at an amusement park. They were on one of their first "holidays" in Europe. Marty was eight and had been walking at Jillian's side. Marty had stopped to look at something at a little gift kiosk, and Jillian hadn't noticed. She kept walking on, but a minute later, when Marty hadn't answered a question she asked her, she realized that Marty wasn't there and went back to look for her.

She expected to find her right away, but everywhere she looked, there was no sign of Marty. Jillian's heart had raced, and she had begun to panic. Tears had gathered in her eyes, just as she noticed some people huddled around someone near some benches. One of the people stepped to the side momentarily, and Jillian caught a glimpse of Marty's bright pink shirt, then ran toward her sobbing daughter. By the time she reached Marty, Jillian was sobbing, too.

She had profusely thanked the people who had tried to help the lost and frightened American child. The whole scene had most likely lasted for five minutes, but it had felt like a lifetime to Jillian.

All kinds of thoughts passed through Jillian's mind—everything from Rick deciding he didn't want to be a part of a family that made him do chores before he could play ball, to the thought that someone had taken him. It was a big city after all, and stranger things than that happened every day.

A police car was parked on the street in front of the house when she arrived. Jillian parked in the driveway and rushed in, throwing her arms around a nearly inconsolable Karen. Robert was recounting the entire morning to an officer, while another looked around the house, taking photos of the "scene."

"Jillian, no one has seen him! Where could he be?" Karen asked between sobs.

"What was he wearing?" the officer asked Robert. Robert looked at Karen for a detailed answer.

"He had on his bright blue Dodgers T-shirt, blue jeans, white and blue sneakers, and a Dodger's baseball cap. We should have just let him play ball!" she said, with guilt and anguish in her voice.

"Karen, don't blame yourself," Jillian said. "Kids get funny ideas sometimes. Maybe there's another explanation." But as soon as she said that, she wished she hadn't. The other possibilities seemed even worse.

The officer said they would send another patrol car around the entire area, and she was also going to call the social worker, since the adoption wasn't legal yet. When those words sunk in, Karen really fell apart.

"Even if we find him, they're never going to let us have him now, are they?" she asked.

"Now, Karen, that's not necessarily true. They are going to find him. You are going to be his mother," Jillian said, suddenly getting one of her feelings again that he was going to be all right. She had nothing to go on really, but her feelings rarely failed her. Instead, she tried to think of places that Rick might go.

Suddenly, Jillian wished that she were back home. "Karen, I think I should go to our house in case Rick decides to go there," she said. Karen nodded. "You might also try the cemetery where his father's grave is located. I don't think he would go there, but one never knows. Or perhaps the shelter—the one where we dropped off Jorge after we had pancakes—the day of Rick's father's funeral," Jillian mentioned as she gathered her things to go. The officer took down the locations of the grave and the shelter on her tablet.

Jillian tried to think of any other places he might go. He only had a small amount of money from an allowance he was currently receiving from Karen and Robert. Karen said that his money was missing, but it wouldn't have been enough to get very far.

Jillian said a prayer while she drove home, and also called Nancy to begin the prayer chain at church.

"Oh, my goodness," Nancy said. "Is that the boy I met Christmas Eve—the one in the purple football jersey—who your friends are going to adopt?"

"That's the one, Nancy," Jillian said, tears flooding her eyes. Rick had been so happy that night at church, so proud of his new Northwestern football jersey with his name on it, a present from her and John.

"Pray not only that we find him, but that this incident doesn't keep Karen and Robert from adopting him," Jillian said.

"I will pray for everyone, Jillian. I think I will call Pastor Jim, too, and tell him what's going on," she replied.

"Thanks, Nancy. I appreciate your prayers and your help."

It was almost noon by the time Jillian got home. She looked carefully up and down the street as she approached the house, but didn't see any bright blue Dodgers T-shirt, unfortunately. She noticed that old silver Buick parked down the street again. She wondered whose it was, and why it was there so often lately.

She was pretty sure that Rick couldn't have gotten onto the grounds, but just in case, she looked all over the house and the front and back yards, but no Rick. She knocked on their household helper Esperanza's door, just to tell her what was going on. The young woman said she would pray for Rick, too, and for his worried family, and said that she would keep an eye out for him.

Jillian went back into the house. It was just after twelve, so she decided to try John's cell number, but there was no answer. The statistics the officer had been telling Robert kept ringing in her head. The longer a child was missing, the more likely it was that they would never be found, or if they were found, it wouldn't be a good outcome.

Jillian took a deep breath, and just prayed that her instincts were right, that he was somewhere—and safe. He might be angry, he might be sad or scared, but she felt deep down that he was okay.

An hour passed, and John came into the kitchen, where Jillian was sitting at the counter, still praying and thinking of places that Rick may have gone.

"Sorry I missed your call...what's wrong?" he asked, noticing her ashen face.

She couldn't answer immediately, so John walked over and held out his hand to her. She took it and, as calmly as she could, relayed the incidents of the morning. John's face paled, and the joy of a great morning at the acting workshop quickly flew out the window.

"I'm so sorry I was gone, sweetheart," he said. "How are Karen and Robert?"

"The way one would expect," she replied. "They are afraid that even if Rick is fine—which I feel he is—this will ruin their plans to adopt him."

"Oh, no. I never thought about that. Let's hope it doesn't come to that," he said, pulling her into a hug.

They stood and held each other for a moment, then Jillian's cell phone went off.

It was Pastor Jim. Jillian was thinking how nice it was for him to call, but it turned out to be even nicer than she anticipated.

"Jillian, I hear your friends are missing a boy," he said.

"Yes, they are. It's been an awful morning, Pastor Jim," she responded.

"Well, it's about to get a lot better, because I happen to have a boy named Ricardo, who likes to be called 'Rick' and apparently likes the Dodgers from the way he is dressed, here at the church," he said. Jillian could almost hear his smile in his voice.

"He's at the church?" Jillian asked, and grabbed John's hand and squeezed it.

"Yes, he is. I came over to look over my sermon notes for tomorrow, and he was sitting in the narthex when I got here. He said he wanted to tell God how sorry he was for something bad he had done. You will most likely want to call his parents right away, and maybe you could come over, too."

"We'll be right there!"

Jillian dialed Karen immediately.

John and Jillian barely beat Karen, Robert, and the police to the church. She and John hugged Rick, then stepped aside with Pastor Jim to let the family cry together for a few minutes.

Then the officer, Karen, Robert, and Rick spent some time talking together to find out what had happened. Rick began to cry as he sat at a table, surrounded by a group of relieved adults.

"I broke the vase," he began, looking up briefly at Karen, and then continued his story between sobs. "The one you said was from your grandmother—the one that was very special. I was playing with the baseball in the house. You both asked me not to do that, and I did it anyway." He was sniffling loudly, so Robert handed him a handkerchief from his pocket, then put his hand on Rick's shoulder.

"Rick, you are more important to us than any vase—or anything or anyone could ever be," Karen said, hugging the boy and trying to console him.

"I thought you wouldn't want me anymore…" he went on, breaking the hearts of everyone within hearing distance.

"There's no way that could ever happen, Rick," Robert said, then hugged the boy. Karen couldn't seem to get any words out of her mouth as tears ran down her face.

Karen looked up and her heart sank. The social worker had arrived. She was a wonderful person, but she had to protect her charges, and Karen was sure she was going to have to take Rick away after this incident.

She asked some questions about what had happened. After hearing the story, she turned and spoke to Rick.

"I'm so glad you are okay, Rick," the woman said, touching his shoulder. "We will all meet tomorrow, but for now, I think you should go home—that is, if you want to."

"I want to. I want to go home," he said adamantly, his eyes brimming with fresh tears.

The police officer finished her report, so happy and relieved to be detailing a happy ending for once. The social worker and the Wilsons set a time to meet the next afternoon. The kind woman thought it was best that everyone calm down a bit before they talked, and Karen and Robert wholeheartedly agreed. They wanted to do whatever they could to help Rick. And they wanted to do whatever it would take to keep the boy they now considered their son.

The next morning Karen, Robert, and Rick sat around the table and had pancakes—Rick's favorite food. Karen was so tired. She just couldn't sleep after all the events of the previous day, and worry over the possibility of losing the chance to adopt kept creeping into her mind.

"What do you want to do now?" Robert asked Rick. "Play catch?"

Playing catch was Rick's favorite thing to do in the world, but instead, he shocked his foster parents with his request.

"Could we go see Pastor Jim?" Rick asked.

"Pastor Jim? At the church?" Karen asked.

"Yes. He said he was going to be there today. That's why he was there yesterday—to practice for this morning. Did you know he has two little boys? They are twins, and they like baseball like me."

Robert looked at Karen, then they looked at the clock. "I think we could make the late service," Karen said. "I'll check on the time. You're sure you want to go to church?"

"Yes. I like it there. It was fun at Christmas. I liked all the singing, and I really like Pastor Jim. I want to meet his little boys, too," Rick said.

"Okay, then. It sounds like a plan," Robert agreed, as he and Rick started to clear the dishes. That was becoming their new tradition—whoever cooked didn't have to clean up, and Karen had made the pancakes.

Robert looked at Karen. She wasn't sure what to make of it all, but she shrugged her shoulders slightly and headed upstairs to get ready.

Jillian had been happily surprised when Karen called her and asked for the time of the late service at church. She and John were happy that they would be able to join the Wilsons at the service, too. They waited in the narthex for the Wilson family to arrive, and smiled as they saw Rick lead the way through the church doors, dressed in his Dodgers jersey. The boy went right up to them and gave them each a hug.

Then Pastor Jim saw them and walked over to say hello. He was in his alb and stole, ready for the second service. He looked around for his wife, Janet, who was ushering their six-year-olds from their Sunday school classroom toward them. They rambled down the hallway, bumping into each other on purpose. Max and Matt were quite the characters. There was never a dull moment with them around.

Pastor Jim introduced everyone. The boys were immediately drawn to Rick, who to them seemed so mature. They loved his Dodgers jersey, and asked if they could sit together in church. Pastor Jim looked wary at that idea, but turned to his wife and said, "I'll let you decide about that one." He headed for the door to the sanctuary, where he would enter in a few minutes.

"We'd better all sit down," Janet said. "If you boys are going to sit by Rick, you have to behave."

"We will," they said in unison. John and Jillian knew from seeing the boys on a regular basis that that was going to be a tall order.

The eight of them all walked in just ahead of Pastor Jim and found an empty pew near the front on the side opposite the pulpit, where they could all sit in a row together. The boys sat down next to Rick, one on each side of him.

John and Jillian thought they witnessed a miracle that morning. Whatever Rick did, or didn't do, the boys followed suit. If he sang, they sang. If he was quiet, they were quiet. If they even tried to begin to talk when they shouldn't be talking, all Rick had to do was look at them, and they immediately stopped. Rick listened to Pastor Jim's sermon, watching him closely. The boys did the same.

On the way out, Rick was happily hugged by Pastor Jim. Then the boys happily hugged their dad. Often, they ran past him, trying to get out of there as quickly as they could.

Janet looked to be in a happy state of shock after the service, and said she hadn't enjoyed a church service that much in years.

"Can Rick come over for lunch?" the boys asked their mother when they got to the narthex.

"I don't know. We will have to ask his parents," Janet said, looking to Karen and Robert.

"I'm sorry, not today, boys. But maybe another time. We have someone coming to our house early this afternoon, and we all need to be there. I'll give your mom our phone number so we can set something up for another day, though," Karen responded.

"Aww, that's too bad," Max and Matt said, again in unison. Then one hit the other on the arm and ran down the hall, with the other giving chase.

"Thank you, Rick, for being such a good role model for my sons this morning," Janet said to him as she turned to follow the boys. "What a good boy you are."

Rick looked so proud at being called that, as did Robert and Karen. Then Pastor Jim came up to him, put his hand on his shoulder, and said something similar to what his wife had just said. Again, Rick and his family just beamed.

"See you again, soon, I hope. We have Sunday School at nine o'clock. You are welcome any time. There's a good-sized class of kids around your age," Pastor Jim said, and patted Rick on the back.

"Thank you, again, Pastor, for yesterday," Robert said, and shook his hand.

"You are welcome. Anytime I can be of help, please let me

know," he responded sincerely.

"We will," said Karen, thankful for the support and for such an affirming morning.

That afternoon, the social worker met privately with Rick, then afterward with Karen and Robert.

"Is this going to ruin our plans to adopt?" Karen asked bluntly as they sat down at the table together. She just couldn't seem to hold it back anymore. It was all she had thought about for twenty-four hours. Even in church that morning, she couldn't shake her concerns. She even found herself praying about the situation—something she wasn't accustomed to doing.

"I don't think so," the woman said. "Not after what Rick just told me."

The social worker went on to relay what Rick had just divulged. Apparently, there was a time when Rick had broken something of his father's in their apartment. His father told him he was no good, that he didn't want him anymore, and locked him in a closet overnight. He had told Rick that he was leaving him there and never coming back.

Karen began to cry when she heard that story. "No wonder he ran away and was so afraid," she said. "Poor Rick!"

"I hope this doesn't keep you and Robert from wanting to adopt him," the social worker continued. "There will be many challenges along the way with this young man. He has been through a lot—probably more than any of us can imagine. There will be other times when you will have to deal with unpleasant and unusual situations."

"We would have to do that with any child. We love Rick," Robert said, getting emotional.

Karen grabbed his hand. "Yes, we love Rick. No matter what. We want him as our son," she said confidently.

"Good. I'm very glad to hear that, because he appears to love you both, too, and wants to be your son," she said, smiling for the first time during the visit. "I will make certain to fully document this incident, and what both he and the two of you have said. Also, this would be a good time for another appointment with his therapist, to process this latest situation."

"We will call his counselor tomorrow morning and see if we can move up his next appointment," Karen said, relief in her voice. Both she and Robert saw the woman to the door, surprising her by hugging her before she left. The overworked woman looked grateful as she headed to her car.

Karen and Robert turned to one another, hugged each other, and then kissed. They heard a little noise coming from above them on the stairs, and realized they were being watched. They looked up at Rick, who must have been listening to the conversation from the top step. They motioned for him to come down. The boy bounded down the stairs, and threw himself into a group hug with his parents-to-be.

Chapter Four

John and Jillian sat in the love seat in the library. They had planned on reading, but instead they just cuddled and rested together. The events of the prior day had taken their toll on them. They were tired, but very relieved that things had worked out so well.

Jillian was thinking about Monica, but decided not to bring up the subject of another crisis situation just then. Instead, she asked John to tell her about his previous day's visit to the Esperanza Workshop. He suddenly perked up, as he talked animatedly about the young actors he had met the day before.

"Brooks and Bobbi are doing a great job with them," he said. "They are all talented, and there are a couple who are very much so, and one that might be in the 'special' category. I would have to see him perform again to know if it was just a good day, or if he's really got it. Brooks said he sees the participants' confidence and self-esteem growing week by week. And everyone was so respectful when I was teaching them. It was really encouraging."

"Everyone needs someone to look up to—a role model. I'm so proud of you for being one, John," she said, hugging the arm he had placed around her even tighter.

"Speaking of role models, how about Rick this morning?"

"That was otherworldly," Jillian responded. "I have never seen the twins so well-behaved."

"I guess that means there's hope for all of us," John said, and turned Jillian's face toward his.

She was just going to make some smart-aleck retort and kiss him, when her phone went off again. It was Pete. All she could think of was how her mother used to say that things came in threes, and sincerely hoped that there was not another panicked parent on the end of the line.

She sat up apologetically. "It's Pete," she said, and noticed that her friend was making a face-to-face call this time.

"Go ahead, answer it," John said, then pulled her back against him as she hit the button and Pete's face appeared.

"Hi, Pete! How is everything going?"

"It's great, Jillian. We just had to call you and show you this. Is John there? He'll want to see it, too. Watch!" the excited new father exclaimed.

Pete turned the phone camera toward Kelly, who was hovering over the twins who were lying on their backs on a soft, brightly colored baby blanket on the floor. She was talking to them, smiling and making faces at them, and they were both smiling and cooing right back at her, their tiny arms and legs moving excitedly.

"Did you see that?" Pete asked, switching the phone back to himself.

"We sure did, Pete! That's wonderful. Just what we needed to see," Jillian said, watching the glowing face of her good friend, a vast difference from the other parental faces she had witnessed the past few days.

"We just thought you'd want to see it. We want to have you over—*soon*. How about some night this week? We are home pretty much every night. Check your schedule and let us know when you can come over—even at the last minute. We'll make something simple, maybe on the grill, and you can play with Gus and Grace," Pete said, turning and smiling at Kelly and the twins again.

"That would be very nice, Pete. We will get back to you soon. Thanks for sharing your beautiful babies and their special moments with us. We appreciate it—more than you could know. It's just what the doctor ordered," she said truthfully.

They said goodbye, and Jillian turned to John and smiled. "Well, how about that?"

He smiled back at her. "Almost as good as seeing you smile," he said, then kissed her softly.

"That's just what the doctor ordered, too."

The next morning John was off to the studio offices for the read-through. Jillian was not "called" to be there, so she decided to check on Monica and was glad that she had.

"They are holding his arraignment this morning. I think they waited until the weekend was over, to see if the young woman survived. So far, she is still alive," Monica reported.

Jillian could only imagine the family of that poor girl. On top of their daughter being seriously injured, the press would be all over the place because she was hit by a celebrity's son. Jillian felt sorry for them, understanding the invasion of privacy all too well.

Jillian herself was still trying to adjust to being the wife of a celebrity, and it only got more challenging the more John's career continued to build steam. She thought about the articles in the tabloids when John was shooting the movie with Monica, and was not relishing the stories that would arise once the press knew that his new movie's love interest was none other than Luz. She could just see the headlines now about how their marriage would be in jeopardy. It could get really ugly, really fast.

Monica was speaking again, bringing Jillian's mind back to the present. "I hate to ask you this, but Ben won't be back until this afternoon. Would you come to the arraignment hearing with me?" Monica asked, sounding frightened and meek, neither of which fit her usual personality.

"I could do that," Jillian found herself saying, and set a place to meet Monica so they could go together.

As she backed out of the garage an hour later, Jillian said a little prayer—for Monica and her son, for the girl he hit and her family, and for herself. She felt like she was in some sort of dream. She was driving to help out her husband's ex-lover, while her husband read through a movie script with one of the sexiest women on the face of the planet. It was a strange morning, to say the least. She was so involved in her thoughts, that she didn't even notice the old silver Buick pull away from the curb and follow her as she drove down the street.

Jillian had never seen Monica look so unkempt and haggard. *The press will just love this,* Jillian thought to herself, as they walked toward the back door of the courthouse. The reporters had been kept to a prescribed area outside, but that didn't stop some of them from trying to get a photo as Monica and Jillian walked toward the building. No cameras would be allowed in the courtroom, but an artist would be drawing the scene.

Some of the paparazzi shouted things to Monica. One asked her who her *girlfriend* was—a distinct emphasis on that word. Others asked where her husband was.

Once inside, Monica and Jillian entered through the heavy doors of the courtroom and walked to the front row. They slid into the thick, slickly varnished wooden bench, right behind the table where the defense attorney and Brent would soon be seated. It reminded Jillian of the pews in the church she attended as a youth, and she suddenly found herself saying a silent prayer.

Finally, Brent was led into the courtroom in a bright orange jumpsuit. Monica stifled a cry at the sight of him. He glanced her way with the saddest and most apologetic eyes Jillian had ever seen. He was a gorgeous young man, a good blend of his father and mother. Brent had his father's thick, wavy brown hair, ruddy complexion, and hazel eyes. He was tall, with his mother's high cheekbones and lanky, Olympic swimmer's body. He had been recruited for a college swim team, but his college career only lasted one season. Jillian wondered if his drinking had anything to do with that. Despite his athletic build, his broad shoulders were slumped, and there was an aura of weakness and shame about him as he took his seat in front of them.

The arraignment was over before they knew it, with Brent being charged with his third DUI and causing bodily injury by a vehicle. He was informed that the charge might be amended if the girl's status should change. The judge also set bail at 1.5 million dollars—cash. Afterward, Brent was led back out of the room by the bailiff, glancing furtively at his mother.

Monica sat dazed for a moment in her seat, then she pulled out her cell phone to call her accountant and explain the situation. Monica turned away from Jillian and spoke quietly, but Jillian still overheard her. "I know we just spent a million dollars, but figure out another way to get this money—now!" She paused, put her hand to her head, and then tacked on, "I'm sorry. Please do what you are able, as fast as you are able," she said, in a much softer tone.

Suddenly, Jillian was pretty certain she knew where the anonymous million-dollar donation to the Esperanza Workshop had come from, but pretended that she had not heard the comment when Monica looked at her.

"Let's get out of here," Monica said. They proceeded to Jillian's white Land Rover, surrounded by officers sent to protect them on the way.

They pulled away from the curb, with a few cars pulling out behind them. One of them was an old, silver Buick.

Jillian looked in the rearview mirror. "Looks like we have company," she said.

"When don't we?" Monica asked tiredly.

Jillian felt bad for her friend. She realized at that moment that she was beginning to think of Monica as a friend for the first time. Jillian just nodded in agreement with Monica.

They were quiet on the way to Monica and Ben's house. Jillian wished she could say thank you to Monica for the donation she was quite sure she had given to their project, but there must have been a reason that she didn't want them to know, so she decided to respect that.

They pulled up to the home in Bel Air, and a gate opened automatically for them, Monica having cued the security company to open it for Jillian's vehicle on her cell phone. The cars stopped behind them, some people jumping out with cameras taking photos of Jillian driving Monica up the driveway as the gate closed behind them.

"Would you stay for lunch?" Monica asked when they got to the top of driveway.

"Okay," Jillian said. She was hungry, and she felt that Monica could use some company. She also thought that some of the press might back off if she didn't come back out right away.

A woman with short, gray hair, and wearing a uniform, was working in the kitchen when they walked in.

"Juliette," Monica said, "this is Jillian. She will be joining me for lunch in the dining room as soon as it is ready."

"Yes, ma'am. It won't be long. I made your favorite macaroni and cheese casserole. I thought you could use some comfort food," Juliette said, and then looked like she wished she hadn't mentioned that, especially in front of a guest.

Monica hesitated a moment. "That was kind of you, Juliette. Is that okay with you, Jillian?"

"That sounds wonderful. I haven't had that in a long time. And yes, it *is* comfort food, Juliette. We *all* need that from time to time," Jillian said, smiling at the considerate house helper.

Jillian enjoyed the tasty casserole, and when Juliette had come out of the kitchen to see if everything was okay with the meal, Jillian asked her if she would be willing to share her recipe. But more than the delicious food, Jillian enjoyed the conversation she had with Monica. They talked about their children, their hopes for them, and the ups and downs of being a parent. After a while, it was difficult for Jillian to believe that this was the same woman who had shamelessly pursued her husband just months before. And for the very first time since meeting Monica, Jillian could understand how John could have once been in love with this woman. Previously, it had been a true mystery to her.

They finished their lunch and topped it off with a healthy dessert of fresh California fruit. The strawberries were exceptionally plump and sweet. They sat back in their chairs, drinking cups of coffee and tea, when Ben walked into the dining room.

Monica put her cup of tea down, and tears immediately started streaming down her face, like someone had turned them on with a faucet. She got up and ran into her husband's arms. They held each other and cried together.

Jillian felt a bit awkward to be privy to such a private moment, yet at the same time, she was happy to witness the genuine love that Monica and Ben still appeared to have for one another.

Kathy J. Jacobson

Monica finally pulled back, starting to regain her composure. "We're being rude," she said to Ben, and turned toward Jillian.

"Ben, I'd like you to meet my friend, Jillian Johnson Romano."

Jillian stood up, and she and Ben walked toward one another. He shook her hand with a strong grip. "Thank you so much, Jillian, for being here, and for helping us," he said sincerely.

"I am glad I was able to be with Monica today. This is an awful situation," she replied.

Monica came to her husband's side, and Ben put his arm around her. "I'm not just talking about this mess with Brent. Thank you for whatever you did up in Alaska," he said, and pulled Monica closer to himself.

Just then Juliette appeared and announced that they had a phone call from their accountant. Jillian felt that this was her cue to leave, so she excused herself and told them that Juliette could show her out. Both Monica and Ben gave her a quick hug, then went to another room to take the phone call.

Juliette showed Jillian to the front door, stopping to pick up the recipe she had written out for Jillian for the macaroni and cheese. Jillian looked at the recipe card in her hand. "Oh—Fontina cheese. I wondered what made it so good. Thank you, Juliette," Jillian said as the woman opened the door for her.

"Thank you, Ms. Romano, for helping this family," Juliette responded. Jillian could tell that Juliette truly cared for Ben and Monica and the boys, and gave her hand a squeeze on her way out of the door.

Jillian wasn't looking forward to meeting up with the paparazzi once the gates opened. Sure enough, they were ready and waiting. One of the men yelled to her. "What did Ben do when he found you with Monica?" Jillian could not believe these people. She just drove forward and didn't answer the man. The gates closed behind her, and she was gone down the street.

She looked in the rearview window to see if anyone was following her, but their attention seemed to be on Monica's home instead. She did notice one vehicle pull away from the other side of the street, however. It turned around in the street to began driving in her direction. It was an older model silver Buick. Suddenly, Jillian felt afraid.

When Jillian got home, she called the security company and told them to keep an extra eye out for the silver car, which had followed her almost the entire way home. The director of security said he would have someone on the night shift go through their security tapes for the last week or so to see if there was anything suspicious on them, and they were going to send one of their officers around a couple of times that night. Of course, there was an extra charge for that, but at this point, Jillian wasn't concerned about the money, only their safety.

The arrangements made Jillian feel a bit better as she pulled out her laptop computer to write. She was falling behind on her chapter for her new book. All the incidents of the past few days had really thrown a wrench into her usual pattern of work, making it difficult to get back into the rhythm of the project. She was so grateful, however, that these things had not happened when she was in the thick of helping Nolan rewrite the movie script, or the next week when they would begin production and she would be on the set.

She looked over her notes from Emma, the young woman who headed up a support group for parents who had pregnancy or infant/toddler losses. Emma herself had miscarried twice, but finally was the mother of a healthy little girl. She had given Jillian a plethora of information, and also names of others who might be willing to share their stories. Her suggestions had been invaluable, and Jillian had cried numerous times after coming home from her interviews.

The stories made her book seem even more needed, however, and the people she had spoken with said it was beneficial to talk about it, and also to think that their stories might help someone else in the future. It seemed to help them make some sort of sense out of their own personal losses.

Hours went by like minutes whenever Jillian wrote. She didn't even hear John come in until he was right behind her. She felt his strong, warm hands begin to massage her shoulders and upper back. He knew how much she liked that. After a minute of enjoying his touch, she put her right hand on his left, and held it.

"You spoil me, Mr. Romano," she said.

"Good," he said, and kissed her cheek.

Jillian looked at the time on the upper right-hand corner of her computer. "Oh, I didn't know it was so late. I'm sorry, I didn't start dinner yet," she said, turning toward him.

"Why don't I call in an order for Asian? You look like you are on a roll with your work. Or I could make something simple."

"You've been working all day, John. Go ahead and order," she said, smiling at him. "It won't take me too long to finish this chapter. I finally had a few uninterrupted hours to work on it, so it's been going very smoothly."

"I'll order and tell them to deliver it in an hour or so. Then I'm going to change clothes and work out for a while. I've been sitting all day," he said.

She watched him walk out of the room, pulling his cell phone out of his pocket. It took everything in her power not to follow him. She always missed him so much when they were apart. Maybe they could take a walk after dinner, as it was a pleasant evening, and she could tell him about the day.

As she thought about going out on the street, the thought of the silver Buick invaded her mind again. She was going to have to tell John about it. It was nice to have had the diversion of a few hours of writing, when she was completely in another world. It had been a nice break from her concerns, even if some of the stories she was writing about were very painful. But now she was back to reality. She wasn't relishing using precious time with her husband bringing up the subject of the silver car, but John had to know.

Jillian waited until they were almost finished eating before relaying the incident with the Buick. She hadn't wanted to spoil John's entire meal and evening.

"Do you think we should call the police?" he asked.

Jillian told him about the security company's plan. It sounded like a good idea for the time being, but they both decided they may have to involve the police if they spotted the car again.

They put their leftovers into the refrigerator and the rinsed dishes into the dishwasher, then headed down the driveway for the street. John was anxious to see if the car was parked there once more. They opened the gates and looked both ways. They walked all the streets near their home, just to make sure it wasn't on one of them. It made them both relax when the car was nowhere in sight.

They held hands as they walked back toward the house. A black SUV drove quickly down their street toward them as they neared their property. It pulled up close, and a man in the passenger seat snapped a photo of them just before they opened the gate to their property.

"Sometimes I'm sorry I introduced you to this kind of life, Jillian," John said, as they watched the iron gate close behind them and walked up the circle drive to the house.

"I think the good far outweighs the bad," she said, squeezing his hand.

"I'm glad you feel that way," he said. "By the way, speaking of good, the rewrites that you and Nolan did on the script...perfect. I'm really proud of you, sweetheart."

"Thank you. I never dreamed I would work on a screenplay. I think I could get used to that," she said honestly.

"I think you might have the opportunity to get used to that," he said, and smiled the grin that always made her feel like a moonstruck teenager.

Chapter Five

Maria threw the last loaves of Italian bread into the oven. It was five a.m., and she had been at her shop in downtown Libertyville for an hour-and-a-half. Her regular baker had called in sick late the night before.

As she closed the oven door she sighed, wiping her sweaty forehead with a flour-covered hand. She hadn't even said good-bye to Tommy this morning when she left the house. He had been sound asleep, and she just didn't have the heart to wake him. He seemed more tired than usual lately, and she was beginning to be concerned that he had a health issue of some sort.

She loved her little shop, but there were times, like this one, when she wondered if she should have taken it on. She was always tired when she was at home, and it seemed like their lives revolved around their work schedules, Alison's musical activities at school, and practice drives with their soon-to-be driver. There didn't seem to be much time for just her and Tommy anymore. She wondered if all the other parents at school felt the same way, or if the situation was just unique to them.

She thought back to two years before. It hadn't seemed to be as much of a problem then, and they had two really active teens at that time. *What happened?* She didn't get to finish that thought as a timer went off for one of her featured desserts. It was one of Tommy's favorites. She decided she would put a few pieces aside and take them home with her as a special treat.

She pulled the pan out of the other oven. "Perfect," she said out loud. But inside, she felt just the opposite.

Tommy woke up alone in the bed. He glanced at the nightstand and saw the note from Maria and sighed. He slowly got up, showered and dressed, and made sure that Alison was up and moving. She wasn't as difficult to awaken as John Anthony had been, thankfully. When his son was asleep, it was almost like a bear in hibernation. Tommy wondered how his boy got himself up and to class each day in college, but he obviously was doing it just fine. John Anthony, a red-shirt freshman on the football team at Northwestern, had gotten straight A's his first semester, while working out with his team and working on the crew of a fall musical production.

He thought about his son. He missed having him around. He missed their talks about sports, theater, and what was going on in the world. He missed hearing him sing in the shower. It seemed like nothing was the same at home anymore. He decided he would call John Anthony later in the morning and see if he could take him out for lunch or a cup of coffee. He needed to hear his voice, and not just on the phone. And he needed one of his bear hugs, too, maybe more than anything else.

Tommy called John Anthony, miraculously reaching him on the first try. His son was walking across campus between classes.

"What's up, Dad?"

"That's what I was going to ask you. The usual here, I guess.

Maybe we could talk about it over lunch—if you have the time?"

"I actually do have some time—just an hour. How about meeting at Cozy's for some noodles?"

"That sounds great. Just give me a time," Tommy said. His calendar was fairly clear until a meeting at three. They set a time, and Tommy felt excited as he put his phone away and got back to work.

The meeting with John Anthony was like a "shot in the arm," as Tommy's mother used to say. He smiled when he thought of his mom and wished that she were still living. He needed to talk to her and get some advice. His father had never been the sort for that. His mom, on the other hand, had been a deep thinker and always seemed to have a well-thought-through solution to just about everything, from how to solve the world's problems to whom he should ask to prom. She was really "spot on" on that one, as his prom date one day became his wife.

John Anthony relayed some exciting news over their noodle and rice dishes. He had just received a call from the quarterbacks coach. He was informed that one of his teammates had just decided to transfer to a college in another conference. The player was one of the top three quarterback prospects for the starting position in the fall. John Anthony had just moved up a notch on the depth chart with that announcement. It had been fun for Tommy to see the excitement in his son's eyes.

The team had just begun their spring practices and would have a scrimmage in a couple of weeks. Tommy, Maria, and Alison all had the event marked on their calendars and were looking forward to it.

The rest of their conversation revolved around John Anthony's classes and talk of Alison and Maria. Tommy told him how his sister was practicing for her driver's test. Then he told him how his mom had to go in for the baker early that morning, to which John Anthony responded, "Poor Mom!" Tommy had nodded in agreement.

Tommy walked into his three o'clock meeting feeling uplifted. He hoped they would stay on track with the agenda, so he could get home and tell Maria and Alison about the latest development in John Anthony's life. His son had given him permission to tell the rest of the family, but no one outside of it yet, as the news hadn't been officially announced.

Two hours later, it was clear that Tommy wasn't going to make it home for dinner that night. He was disappointed as he hit Maria's contact number. It went to voicemail, so he left a message, telling her he didn't know when he would be home that evening.

At seven o'clock, the meeting finally ended. He went to his office to retrieve his suit jacket and head for home when Amanda Richards appeared in the doorway. Even after a long meeting, the woman still managed to look like she was on her way to a modeling session.

"It looks like your leaving," she said in a sweet voice. "I was hoping we could go over some ideas together."

"I really should get home, I've already missed dinner…"

"I could order in—my treat," she said.

Tommy thought better of it, but he still found himself saying, "Sure," as he put his suit jacket back over the chair back and sat down.

Amanda took out her phone and asked if he had any food preferences. He shook his head "no." He was so hungry by this time that he didn't really care what was set in front of him.

They started in on their plan for a new mixed-use building.

They would be meeting with architects soon, but were trying to decide on the best businesses to complement one another, and best serve and fit the neighborhood in which it would be built.

They made some lists, using the smart board on Tommy's office wall. The food arrived, along with some heavy paper plates and plastic utensils.

"Let's take a break. I'm starving," Tommy said.

They sat at a small round table in the corner of his office. He felt self-conscious suddenly, being so close to Amanda and eating together. He wished he were at home, telling his wife and daughter about John Anthony. Instead, he found himself telling Amanda.

"Oh, that is so exciting," she said in a sweet tone that she never seemed to use with anyone other than Tommy. "You must be so proud of him."

"I am." He pulled out his phone, showing her a recent photo of John Anthony.

"So handsome!" she exclaimed, and then tacked on, "Like his father."

Tommy could feel the blood rushing to his face. "Actually, I think he's a combination of my wife and my uncle John," he said, trying to dismiss her comment.

"Your uncle must be very handsome, then," she replied.

"He is considered to be, I guess. He's an actor. In fact, he won an Oscar a few months ago for Best Supporting Actor."

"Your uncle won an Academy Award? Who's your uncle?" she asked in an amazed voice.

"John D. Romano," he said proudly.

"Oh, my mom used to love him when he was on that T.V. show—what was it called?"

"O.R.," he answered.

"That's the one," she said. "I'll have to tell her. I'll Google him later, too, to check out that award. Good looks and talent seems to run in your family, don't they?"

Again, he felt a new wave of heat in his face. He quickly suggested that they get back to work, almost knocking over a carton of food as he stood up abruptly from the table. He helped straighten it, and then walked over to the smart board once more.

Tommy couldn't wait to get out of there. It wasn't that Amanda wasn't a nice person. She *was* nice—*too* nice. It had been a long time since Tommy had felt pursued by a member of the opposite sex. The last time was in college, but he was already engaged to Maria. He hadn't had this kind of experience in a really long time. It felt strange. It also felt flattering—and that scared him to death.

Tommy got home about nine-thirty. He was beat, physically and emotionally. Alison was sitting at the kitchen table, studying and eating a piece of her mother's tiramisu.

Tommy came up behind his daughter and gently put his hands on her shoulders.

"Hmmm," he said, "that looks good."

"The dessert or the book?" Alison asked in a smart tone.

"Well, I was referring to the dessert, but is the book equally wonderful?" he asked.

"The book is lame. The dessert—nothing's as good as Mom's tiramisu, except maybe Leo's in California," she said. "There's a piece for you in the refrigerator. Mom's reading in the den, I think."

"Thanks, I'll check it out," he answered, and gave her shoulders one last squeeze before he left her.

He hung up his overcoat and laid his briefcase by the front door. Before he knew it, he would be heading back out the same door. He hated getting home so late from work.

He washed his hands, found the piece of dessert waiting for him in the refrigerator, and walked into the den. The light was on, and Maria sat with a book laying open on her chest, sound asleep. She looked angelic when she slept. Tommy had always thought that. He sat down gently next to her on the couch, and her eyes slowly opened.

"Hi, honey," she said sweetly, and smiled at him. Her eyes brightened as she focused on his face. "I'm sorry, I guess I dozed off."

"That's okay. I hope your baker is feeling better," he replied.

"He is. I talked to him tonight," she said. "He will be in tomorrow morning, thank goodness."

Then Tommy remembered to tell her about John Anthony's news, feeling guilty that his co-worker Amanda knew about it before his own wife. Worse yet, John Anthony had asked him not to tell anyone but their family.

"I'll bet he's so excited. You should have called me," she said.

"I wanted to tell you in person. I never dreamed that I would be at the office so late. The change in this new project is really going to create a lot more work for us, I'm afraid. It would have been so simple had they stayed with their original plan," Tommy said, not relishing the extra hours that it would entail.

"Good thing they hired another associate," she answered sincerely. "What's her name again—Angela?"

"Amanda," he said, feeling color rising to his face.

"I knew it began with an 'A,'" she said. "I'm happy that you won't have to do everything by yourself."

He changed the subject by telling his wife how much he loved her dessert, as he set the empty dish and fork down on the coffee table in front of them. When he leaned back in the couch, Maria put her head on his shoulder, and he put his arm around her instinctively, like he had been doing for the past twenty-two years, ever since their first date on the night of the prom. As he held her familiar form, his mind drifted back to work. Tommy wished his company had never hired Amanda Richards.

Kathy J. Jacobson

Chapter Six

Greta's stomach was churning that morning as she got ready for her study group. She couldn't wait to be done with her degree. She had wisely finished her dissertation just before spring break and had successfully defended it. It had been difficult to do that as a newlywed, but she knew that ultimately she would be grateful that she had. Indeed, it had been a good plan.

She had several interviews set up in the next two weeks for positions teaching art at two community colleges and one small university in the area. She was excited about all of them, especially now that she was "geographically restricted" to the Los Angeles area because of Drew's work. She didn't want to live away from her husband of only five months.

As soon as graduation was over and she knew where she would be teaching, they would decide if they would stay in the house Drew had owned for years or would buy or build a new home between his work and hers. She didn't really care where she lived, as long as it was with Drew.

She sometimes thought of the arrogant, self-centered accountant she had met by chance when she was working as a personal trainer at the gym. He had been signed up to have a session with a different trainer, Pete, but Pete had taken time off to get ready for his wedding. Greta was assigned to Drew instead at the last minute. When they first met, Greta could barely stand him, and the feeling had been mutual. Then, miraculously, he had asked her to coffee one day. She had suggested her favorite indie coffee shop, thinking he would turn her down or not show up at the last minute.

But he had accepted—and showed up—and her view of Drew, and her life, had been changed in a matter of hours. He had been a good surprise, and he kept on growing into an even better one on a daily basis. She thought about the man he was becoming, slowly but surely, and how much she loved him more and more each day. She also loved the way he loved her, making her feel so very special.

She grabbed her backpack, and her head went reeling for a second. Another wave of nausea came over her, and she ran to the bathroom.

"Great! This is just what I need with finals and interviews coming up," she said sarcastically.

She slapped water on her face, brushed her teeth, and headed out the door to her study group. She wasn't going to blow this now, with graduation right around the corner. She was going to finish well, so no excuses.

It was a miserable day for Greta, although she felt a bit better as the day wore on. At least she wasn't as queasy as she had been in the morning. She thought about what she had eaten, and decided that she was going to purge the refrigerator when she got home, in case something in it was expired. She was very tired, so she suspected that it was the flu, but just in case, she wasn't taking any chances.

She stopped and shopped for a few items at the store on her way home. She would replace the items she always insisted on having on hand, planning to throw the ones at home away.

She walked by a store employee who was giving away free samples of pizza—one of her favorite foods—and another wave of nausea hit her again. *What in the world is going on with me?*

She walked down an aisle filled with medicinal and personal care items, looking for an antacid, when a thought suddenly popped into her mind.

No—it couldn't be—could it? She looked at the shelves, and indeed, the store did carry pregnancy tests. She looked around like she was guilty of something, then threw the small rectangular box into her cart. She'd wasted more money than that on things she had bought in the past. She just wanted to put her mind at ease. She didn't need any other stresses invading her mind during this final stretch of her educational career.

An hour later, Greta stared in disbelief at the "positive" sign glaring at her from the plastic test cylinder. She read the instructions once again. It said that all tests should be confirmed by a physician, and gave the percentages of a false positive.

It must be wrong. It can't be right.

The next day, she walked by the student health clinic on campus on the way back from her exam and decided she had to know, one way or the other. She went inside and asked about a test. After waiting for an hour, she was tested. Another hour later, she walked out in a daze. She was pregnant.

It was Friday night, and Drew came home early. He had been working hard to do that ever since they had gotten married, trying to overcome some of the workaholic behaviors he had developed over the years.

"Hi, hon," he said, wrapping his arms around Greta. "Are you feeling any better tonight?"

Greta wasn't certain how to respond. She wasn't sure what Drew would think about this. They had talked about having children, and they both seemed to want some—or at least one—but she wasn't planning on starting a family quite this soon.

She didn't answer him at first. She was trying to think about how to say it, and tears began to gather in her eyes.

"Greta, what's wrong?" Drew asked in a concerned voice.

Greta sat down at the table. He sat next to her, taking her hand in his. Then she told him the news. He looked surprised for a moment, then a huge smile crossed his face. "Really?"

She nodded. "I took one of those home pregnancy tests yesterday, and today I stopped at the student health center and checked to make sure it wasn't a mistake."

"We're going to have a baby?" he asked in a tone of disbelief. Then another smile crossed his face and he said, "We're going to have a baby!" He stood up and pulled Greta into his arms and held her.

All she could do was hold on, as tears trickled down her face.

Greta sat in the plush chair in the living room, staring out the window and thinking. The past two weeks had been a blur. On top of exams, she had gone to three job interviews. The last one was her favorite, and she hoped that she would be offered the position. Her only concern was how the school would react when it found out that its new professor was pregnant.

Her final exam went well—or so she thought. She could barely concentrate on anything other than the fact that they were pregnant. They planned to tell their families and friends the next day at graduation. Greta had already seen her family doctor, who also confirmed that she was almost six weeks into her pregnancy. She still felt awful every morning, but usually felt better as the day progressed. She had also learned what foods to avoid, including her beloved cup of coffee. She couldn't even stand the smell of it.

Greta still couldn't believe the pregnancy was real. She wondered how she was supposed to feel. Drew seemed to be walking on air. She felt like crying most of the time, but she had read that hormones could cause all types of mood swings, so she felt that must be the reason. She tried to put the entire issue out of her mind, but it wasn't that easy to do. There was a human being growing inside her, and it was a completely foreign experience. She felt confused and uncertain. She wondered if she would feel differently if this hadn't been so unexpected.

Just then Drew walked through the door with a stuffed animal under his arm and a huge smile on his face. She forced a smile in return, pretending to feel as excited as he was. He hugged her, and she was glad that he couldn't see the expression on her face.

The stage felt like it was moving as Greta walked across it. Why did she have to wear this heavy hood? It felt like she had a saddle on her back, and it seemed like it was one hundred degrees outside rather than the actual temperature of seventy-five. She walked toward the Dean of Students, feeling a bit wobbly, but she made it. She shook her hand, grabbed her diploma, and headed straight to the nearest restroom.

Greta wished the ceremony had been in the afternoon rather than the morning, but there were many graduations that day and her department was part of one of the earlier ceremonies. She couldn't wait for the day to be over so she could go home and take a nap. She had never been so tired in her entire life.

After the ceremony, she joined Drew, her parents and his, and

John and Jillian by the sculpture of the UCLA Bruin. Greta, then Drew and Greta, then the entire family posed for photos of the happy occasion, with Jillian playing photographer. Greta found it difficult to smile. She didn't feel well, and hoped that she didn't look as green on the outside as she felt on the inside.

As soon as they were done with the photos, they got out of the way for other graduates to have a turn. Greta quickly peeled off the graduation gown, cap, and hood. She would keep her vestments for graduation ceremonies at whatever school she was given a position—that is, if she was offered one.

"Are you okay, dear?" Drew's mother asked, as Greta handed the garments to Drew. She wanted to scream "no!" Instead she nodded, and looked to her husband for help. Drew smiled and pulled Greta to his side.

"Moms, Dads, and good friends, we are going to have a baby!" he said proudly.

Hugs and words of congratulations were offered, but Jillian could sense, and could see in Greta's eyes, that she was struggling with all of this. As they all walked toward their cars to go back to Drew and Greta's for a cookout, she took the younger woman by the arm.

"It's a bit overwhelming, isn't it?" Jillian asked quietly.

Greta nodded, and tears filled her eyes.

"We weren't expecting...to be expecting...not yet anyway," Greta answered quietly.

Jillian, of all people, knew how that felt—big time. She squeezed Greta's arm and gave her an understanding look. "Let's talk sometime soon," she said as they approached the cars. Greta nodded in agreement and gave her a small smile.

John and Jillian returned to their home mid-afternoon. They had been the first to leave, after Jillian made the comment that Greta needed her rest. Luckily, both sets of parents seemed to be willing to follow suit, and Greta had given Jillian a very grateful look as they headed out. The young woman was clearly exhausted.

John and Jillian had just changed into comfortable clothes and sat down in the library when the buzzer went off signaling that someone was at the front gate.

They both sighed, but John jumped up first. "My turn," he said.

Jillian could hear him talking with whomever it was on the intercom, then he appeared at the doorway of the room.

"I think you're going to like this one," he said, smiling, and motioned for her to join him at the front door.

A minute later, there was a knock on the door. John opened it, and there stood Marty, a backpack slung over her shoulder.

"What a great surprise," John exclaimed as he hugged his soon-to-be legal daughter.

Jillian looked at her daughter's face. She didn't see the familiar smile or bright eyes, and immediately wondered what was wrong.

It was her turn to hug her sweet daughter. She held her extra tight, and Marty responded. Something was definitely "up," but they would talk about that in a bit. She took Marty's backpack from her, then they all began to naturally head for the kitchen. For whatever reason, that seemed to be the place many families spend much of their time, talking and working things out, and theirs was no exception.

Jillian gave John a concerned look as Marty started down the hall in front of them toward the kitchen. He read her face immediately, and as they entered the kitchen, he asked if it was all right if he made one quick phone call before he joined them. Jillian adored this perceptive and thoughtful man. Marty and Jillian both said "okay" at the same time, and mother and daughter slid into the benches of the breakfast nook.

"Would you like something to drink, honey?" Jillian asked.

"Just some water," Marty responded.

Jillian scooted back out and walked to the sink, filling two glasses with filtered water. They both liked their water without ice, having learned to enjoy it that way while living in Tanzania. Even soda pop was often served at room temperature there, as few had refrigeration.

Jillian put the glasses down on the table and sat directly across from Marty.

"Well, you are in the middle of final exams and you are here. I'm guessing this is more than just a social visit. What's up?" Jillian asked her daughter.

"I heard back about the residencies. I was accepted at all of the hospitals," she said.

"And Michael?"

"So was he."

"That's good, isn't it?" Jillian asked.

"I thought it was—until he told me he really wants to accept the one in Peru," she said, her eyes filling with tears.

"He must have his reasons," Jillian remarked.

"He said he wants to be involved in studying and fighting the Zika virus, and helping those affected by it," Marty said.

"Very important work," Jillian said.

"Yes, I know it is," Marty said, "but I always thought I'd go back to Africa. I've wanted to work there since...well, I guess I don't have to tell you that, Mom."

Jillian felt sorry for Marty. Her daughter had been talking about curing diseases on the African continent since she was ten years old. Marty had lived in two African nations and loved them both.

"These will be difficult decisions—for both of you," Jillian said. "Will one of you go somewhere that's not your number

one choice? Or do you want to spend three years apart? Or..."
She didn't finish her sentence.

Marty looked distraught. "I just never thought I'd have to make this decision," Marty said. "I thought Michael and I were on the same page, but I guess I was wrong. It just took me by surprise."

It was the second time that day that Jillian had heard those sentiments. Sometimes surprises were wonderful. Other times they were not. Sometimes they don't start out that great, but they turn out to be very special. Jillian was sitting across from a prime example of that latter type of surprise—Marty.

Jillian reached across the table and held her daughter's hands. "You have a good head and a good heart," she said, "and so does Michael. I am sure you will work it out."

"I sure hope so," she replied, looking so sad it hurt Jillian's heart.

Just then, John came into the room. He looked at Jillian as if to ask if it was okay to intrude. She smiled at him and nodded her head slightly. He came and sat down with them at the table.

"How long can you stay, Marty?" John asked. He was kind enough not to make her repeat everything she had just told Jillian.

"My next exam is on Wednesday, so I'll have to leave very early on Tuesday. I have all my books and computer with me so I can study."

They talked for a bit about the exams she had already taken and the two that were left.

Marty sighed, suddenly looking very tired.

"Would you mind if I took a shower? " Marty asked. "I feel grimy from the bus."

"Go ahead, honey," Jillian said.

"Thanks, Mom. It's okay if you fill Dad in on what's going on." Then she turned to John. "If that's all right with you?" she said, wearily while rising from her seat.

John nodded that it was okay, and hugged her. "What would

you like for dinner, Marty?" he asked.

"Comfort food," she said matter-of-factly.

"I know just the thing," he said, and hugged her again.

After Marty left the room, Jillian gave John the details of the conversation as he started preparing his mother's recipe for gnocchi.

"That's a difficult one," he said. "There are no simple answers. At best, one of them will not be getting what they want. At worst, they will both be thousands of miles apart and miserable without one another, or..." He didn't finish the sentence, just as Jillian hadn't when speaking with Marty. The "or" was that they simply went their separate ways.

"Let's hope it doesn't come to 'or,'" Jillian said.

The comfort food definitely helped ease the pain of the day. Marty was even able to talk some about the residency programs and places, including the one in Lima, Peru. She talked about the facilities, faculties, and projects each was working on, and how the emphasis had recently changed in South America because of the Zika outbreak.

They also discussed the upcoming adoption proceedings, which Robert had gotten moved up to the next month. In a very wise move, he had asked if the Romanos minded sharing a judge. Marty and Rick would both become legally adopted on the same day. There would be two very happy families celebrating together, and they couldn't wait.

All the positive talk lifted Marty's mood.

"I wish I could have met my other grandma," Marty said, as she helped put away the little bit of gnocchi that was left.

John looked very touched by her words. "I wish she could have met you, too, Marty—and your mom. She would have loved you

Kathy J. Jacobson

both so much. And she would have been so happy for me."

Marty had a lot of studying to do, so she had to excuse herself to her suite. Before she headed up, she turned around and hugged each of them again, and told each of them that she loved them.

"I'll see you both in the morning," she said. "What service are we going to?"

"How about the late one?" Jillian suggested.

"I was hoping you would say that," Marty said, sounding thankful for a later wakeup time.

John watched her leave and then turned to Jillian. He pulled her into his arms. "What did I ever do to deserve a daughter like that?"

"Let me know if you come up with an answer, John. I've been asking myself that for twenty-six years."

His face turned more serious. "I wasn't expecting something like this to happen to Marty," John said.

"Neither was I, but I have learned as a parent over the years, to expect the unexpected. It's too bad this is all happening in the middle of finals," Jillian remarked.

"I'm going to find her a flight home on Tuesday. Enough of that bus business," John said.

"For someone who's a new dad, you're pretty good at it," Jillian said, pulling him close.

"I'd bet our daughter is asking the same thing about you, that you were asking about her."

He smiled at the compliment. "Speaking of new dads, how about Drew and Greta?"

"I've never seen Drew so happy. And I've never seen Greta so down. I told her we would talk sometime this week. Pregnancy can be a bit daunting. I think she just needs to talk," Jillian said.

"Well, if anyone can help her, I'm sure it would be you. You're the best, Mrs. Romano," he said, looking at her lovingly with those chocolate brown eyes.

There would have been a time when Jillian would have argued with him, but she was slowly and surely learning how to take a compliment.

"Thank you, Mr. Romano," she said, and gave him a kiss to remember.

Chapter Seven

Sunday was quiet, particularly in comparison to the drama of the previous day. As usual, the church service left everyone feeling more hopeful and ready for the week. John, Jillian, and Marty stopped for soup and sandwiches at Buck and Nancy's new condo on the way home, avoiding the public restaurant scene. The couple's new place wasn't far from the church, and Buck and Nancy stayed there almost every Saturday night, unless Buck's weekend foreman was gone from the ranch for some reason.

At last, Nancy had been willing to part with the house she and her first husband had bought together many years before. It was a tough decision, but she was gradually adjusting. They were only renting the property at this point, but they were considering buying it and making it an investment property.

Nancy was enjoying the large kitchen with its new appliances and endless counters and cupboards. She loved to cook, so it was perfect for that. Her grandkids were thrilled with the tennis courts and swimming pool on the grounds, which could be used by guests of the residents.

Nancy's children and grandchildren had been wonderful at

supporting her decision to sell the house, which made it easier for everyone. They all liked Buck. He was a genuinely nice man, and they especially loved how happy he made Nancy. Also, her grandchildren had never known their biological grandfather because of his death at a very young age. They enjoyed having a grandpa for the first time, and Buck seemed equally happy to fill that role.

Buck had mentioned to John over lunch that he wanted to come down and see what was going on at the Esperanza Workshop "one of these days." He had an appointment in the city later that week, and wondered if he could get a tour. John looked at his schedule, and they made plans for a six o'clock tour on Thursday. John told him he would meet him just inside the building. John was excited to show his friend the new classroom and the stage which was being built with the generous donations that had come in, and mentioned the one for a million dollars, wondering once more who could have been responsible.

Buck said that if he had it, he would have given it. He and Nancy had made a very generous donation themselves, but not too many people were in a position to make a contribution as large as a million dollars. Jillian smiled inwardly as she thought she knew the answer to the puzzle, but had decided to forever hold her peace, unless the donor decided to come forward on her own. Besides, she couldn't say for certain that it was Monica.

After lunch at Buck and Nancy's, it was more studying for Marty, swimming for John and Jillian, then running lines for the next day's filming at the studio. Jillian looked at the script and sighed. She realized that she wasn't going to enjoy the next day's shoot very much, as there was the bedroom scene with John and Luz. She still couldn't believe Carson had put her in this situation, but she guessed that was showbiz. She knew the scene well. She had helped craft it, tweaking it to a reasonable level from Nolan's first few drafts. Still, it would make the next day an uncomfortable one.

John and Jillian went together to the studio very early Monday morning. Jillian planned to use the first hour or so to work on her book on her laptop while John and the other actors were in makeup.

John was just saying goodbye to Jillian when Luz appeared, bubbly and spewing "good mornings" to everyone as she entered the area. It was 5:30 a.m., and the woman looked amazing. This time she was in a tight-fitting, bright yellow sundress, with a very revealing cut. Her brilliant white-toothed smile stood out against her dark skin and jet-black hair. Jillian wondered why she should have to go to makeup, as it would be hard to improve on what appeared to be natural perfection. It was difficult to keep one's eyes off of this woman, no matter who you were. It was like there was a magnet drawing one's eyes to her.

John squeezed Jillian's hands and gave her a deep and loving look. "See you on the set, sweetheart," he said, and walked into the room to his chair, followed by a smiling Luz.

Once out of makeup, they worked on a medical office scene. Then it was time for the dreaded bedroom scene. Jillian, although she had watched John crawl between the sheets with Monica Morgan just months before, felt that she needed to take a breather from this one. She excused herself to take her contracted break and went to another part of the studio. Just imagining the scene was bad enough—she didn't need to witness it.

After forty-five minutes, Carson Stone came around the corner. "There you are," he said.

"Oh, sorry, did you call for me? I don't have a notification on my phone," Jillian asked, glancing down at her cell phone.

"No, I didn't," he said, sitting down next to her at the small table where she was sitting.

"I would imagine the last scene was not one of your favorites—to write or to watch," he said.

Jillian was getting fairly comfortable around Carson. He wasn't the gruff, impersonal man so many people thought he was. Actually, she found him intelligent, thoughtful, crazy talented, and charming at times.

"That would be an understatement. It doesn't help that you picked the most beautiful person on the planet, Carson," she said honestly.

"She is a stunning woman," he agreed with an unusual look on his face.

"Again, that would be an understatement. If I didn't know better, I would think you were trying to ruin my marriage. First, it was Monica Morgan, and now Luz," Jillian said.

"Jillian, I don't think that would be possible. I've been around many, many Hollywood couples for a long time now. I've never seen the kind of relationship that you and John share. It is *stunning* in its own way. If anyone's marriage can survive this, yours can."

Jillian was surprised by his words. "Thank you. I do think it's special, and I trust John..."

He cut her off mid-sentence. "You don't know how lucky you are to be able to trust like that," he said, with a hint of sadness in his voice. "Anyway, are you ready to get back to work?"

"You bet," she replied, closing up her laptop. She stood, and they walked back to the set together, with Jillian feeling a new kind of admiration for Carson Stone.

The next scene was another "house scene," but no longer in a bedroom, instead in a kitchen. John and Luz were wearing robes and sitting at the breakfast table, discussing the trafficking of internal organs for transplants. The movie really was an important one, so it helped Jillian remember why she had agreed to sign on to the project in the first place.

After Carson called it a wrap, the actors started for their dressing rooms, with John going one direction, Luz in the other.

As Luz walked near Jillian she stopped to talk to her. "May I speak with you—in private?" she asked, looking around to see who might be listening.

"Certainly," Jillian responded, but feeling uncertain inside. She couldn't imagine what Luz would want to speak to her about.

They came to Luz' dressing room, and Luz invited Jillian inside. It was a spacious room with a sitting area. Luz indicated that Jillian should sit down. She wondered if Luz had a problem with the script that she wanted to talk about.

Luz spoke quietly. "Your husband..."

Jillian's eyes flashed at the words, and Luz must have noticed.

Luz put her hand on Jillian's arm. "There is not a problem, Mrs. Romano," she said.

"Your husband is one of the most kind, gracious, and respectful men I have ever worked with," she said. "I can't tell you how disgusting some actors can be. But Mr. Romano—he treats me like a human being, rather than an object." As she said this, her eyes grew moist.

Jillian let out the breath she hadn't realized she had been holding. "Yes, he is very special. I am so glad you are having a good experience working with him, Luz."

"I hope someday I can find someone who would love me for who I am, rather than for my...appearance...or the kind of woman they think I am," she said.

Jillian thought for a moment about what Luz had just said. "Luz, I don't mean to be disrespectful, but if you want to change some of that, there could be some ways you could discourage some of that behavior and change some of that perception."

"How?"

"First of all—by the way you dress. Tight dresses with a lot of cleavage don't help matters any," she said honestly, trying not to sound like the biggest prude on earth.

"I know, but my agent says I need to dress like that. He says I have an image to uphold," she replied.

"But you don't seem very pleased with that image. And perhaps it is attracting the wrong types of men and an incorrect impression of the woman you truly are," Jillian said.

"Perhaps. I certainly have not had a good experience with men," she said, looking down. "My last boyfriend...we were together for two years. I loved him, but he...hit me."

"I hope he is far away from you now?" Jillian asked.

"Yes, he is back in Lima. He owns a mansion in the La Molina district. He is a very influential and wealthy man, and I cared for him...but not anymore. Once he started abusing me, I left. I worked too hard to get away from that type of life. My father..." she said, her voice trailing off.

"Is that where you are from?" Jillian asked, trying to change the subject.

"I am from the Lima city area, but not La Molina. I grew up in Ate—it's spelled liked your English word 'ate,' but is pronounced 'AH-tay.' It's an entirely different world in Ate than in La Molina... I shouldn't be going on and on. I just wanted you to know that you need not worry about me and Mr. Romano. I noticed that you left when we had our...scene...today. I just wanted you to know that he was a gentleman...and you are a very fortunate woman," Luz said.

"Yes, I know that, but thank you for your words. And I hope that you will find someone who sees you, and loves you, for who you really are," Jillian told her.

"Me, too. Maybe I'll start wearing what I really like to wear,"

Kathy J. Jacobson

Luz said.

"What is that?"

"Blue jeans!" Luz said with a huge, brilliant smile.

Jillian smiled back, and suddenly had a thought. "Luz, what are you doing for dinner this evening? Would you like to come to our home and have dinner with John, our daughter, Marty, and me? You can wear blue jeans... we won't tell anyone!"

"Really? I would love to come to your house for dinner!" Luz exclaimed.

Jillian gave her the address and a time.

The two women hugged, and Jillian headed out to meet John in the cafeteria for lunch.

"I hope you don't mind," Jillian said to John as they sat down at a tall table, "but I just invited Luz to our house for dinner tonight."

John looked a bit surprised at first. "That's fine—but I hope you don't mind, I just invited Carson to our house for dinner tonight, too," he said with a smile on his face. "He seemed a bit down this morning, and the idea just came to me."

"Great minds think alike," she replied. Then she put her hand on his gently. "By the way, I was reminded just a few minutes ago by Luz about what a very lucky woman I am."

"That's interesting. I was reminded a few minutes ago by Carson about what a lucky man I am," he said.

She smiled at him. "I suppose we had better warn each of them that the other is coming. Also, we're going to go really informal. Luz is going to wear blue jeans, and so am I," Jillian said.

"Okay, I will tell Carson. Maybe we should make some burgers on the grill," he said.

"Our daughter would most likely enjoy that—with some French fries!" she said, remembering how much Marty had enjoyed those foods after her appetite finally returned after suffering from Dengue Fever in Senegal. John had had them delivered to her home from a restaurant in Dakar, much to Marty's delight.

"It sounds like a plan," he agreed. "I'll call in an order to the grocery store." They had been having home grocery deliveries more and more often. The paparazzi were making life more and more difficult for normal store shopping as John's career continued its upward trajectory. Fame, it appeared, came with a price.

Luz and Carson arrived within minutes of each other, both wearing blue jeans. John and Jillian had never seen either of them in such wardrobe selections before. It was a fun and unusual transformation. Jillian did note that Luz could make jeans look better than anyone else she had ever known. She was happy that Luz truly felt comfortable enough to take her up on the invitation to dress the way she enjoyed, not the way her agent wanted her to dress. Jillian thought that perhaps it was time for Luz to get a new agent.

For the next three hours, the five diners enjoyed each other's company. The "burger bar," complete with grass-fed Angus, turkey, and veggie burgers, and every type of topping one could imagine, was a huge hit. Jillian decided that French fries were too risky—they never seemed to turn out the way she wanted them to turn out. Instead, she made her mom's recipe of potato salad, along with a few other salads that had a definite Midwestern flare to them. And of course, there was plenty of cheese. She and Marty kidded about being "Cheeseheads," and Marty showed Luz a photo of them together at the one Packer game they had attended when Marty was in college, wearing the famous yellow foam wedges on their heads.

Luz thought it was fabulous, and said she wanted to visit

Kathy J. Jacobson

Wisconsin and wear one someday. That brought up the subject of people's home territories. Carson said he was from a small town in North Dakota. He said he left when he was nineteen and never looked back. John and Jillian were both surprised. They both assumed he was a native Californian for some reason. Then Luz talked about Lima. Marty's ears perked up when she heard "Lima," and the two of them proceeded to talk at length about Luz' country and its capital city.

Carson seemed the most relaxed they had ever seen him, except when Luz spoke directly to him. He was usually a great conversationalist and used impressive-sounding words from his extensive vocabulary. He didn't do it to impress, but because that was just Carson. But when Luz spoke to him, he seemed to lose his concentration and words, and answered in short, simple answers. He wasn't rude—he was just different—almost timid—and timid was not a word one associated with Carson Stone—ever.

He did smile whenever Luz said something witty, which was often. She was really a fascinating person—bright, and with a good sense of humor. Jillian was so glad they were all having this special opportunity to get to know one another and found it serendipitous that both she and John had invited guests home on the same evening, and one who was from Lima, Peru, no less. It felt like what Nancy often called such a coincidence—a "God-cidence."

A little before ten, Luz pulled out her phone to call for her car, but Carson stopped her. He had driven over in his own vehicle and offered her a ride home, which she gladly accepted. They all hugged each other good night in the circle drive, promising to do this again sometime soon. Carson surprised them once more by saying that maybe he would cook next time.

As John and Jillian put away food and Marty began to wash the dishes, everyone was quiet. It had been a pleasant, but very long day. Marty was flying home the next morning at ten a.m. A taxi would be picking her up early, so soon she would pack her backpack, get ready for bed, and look over her notes for her exam one more time.

"I'm really glad I came here," Marty said before she went upstairs for the night.

"So are we," John and Jillian said in unison, then laughed.

John hugged and kissed Marty goodbye, as he would most likely not see her in the morning. Jillian would go in to the studio with her own vehicle later than John, so she could make certain that Marty was up and ready to go. There could be no snafus at exam time.

After Marty retired for the night, John and Jillian finished up in the kitchen and looked around.

"It's as good as it's going to get," Jillian said.

"Esperanza will be in tomorrow. If we missed anything, she will get it," John said, coming up to Jillian and pulling her close.

"You are right. She's an eagle-eye when it comes to discovering dirt and deep-cleaning. I never got things to shine the way she does," Jillian remarked.

"Maybe not, but you have other qualities that are appreciated," he said, nuzzling her neck.

"The alarm's going to go off pretty early," she said, as he kissed her ear next.

"I guess we'd better get to bed then," John suggested.

"Okay—if you insist."

Chapter Eight

B rent Bastien was uncuffed by the guard, and walked straight into the waiting arms of his parents. As they embraced, he began to sob, and Ben and Monica followed suit. Their accountant had come through with the 1.5 million dollars in cash needed for his bail, and Brent's trial date was set in six weeks. In the meantime, Brent was finally going home. The past week had seemed like a lifetime, and a living nightmare.

Ben had told his agent he would not be auditioning for anything else until this ordeal with his son was over. Their first priority was Brent, and their other son, Bart. Bart would be joining them at home that evening for dinner. It would be the first time the family had all been together for a meal since their week in Antigua several months before, and the first one together at the family's residence in over a year.

Juliette was out of her mind with excitement. She was making "the boys"—which is the way she still thought of them—their favorites tonight. The main course was her specialty, lasagna, with Caesar salad with homemade dressing on the side. Best of all, she had baked brownies for dessert—one pan with nuts for Brent, one without for Bart. She had ordered their favorite brand of vanilla ice cream to be delivered, and made her own hot fudge sauce to top it all off.

Bart arrived shortly after the other family members arrived home from the jail. Their meal would be early, as Bart's "call" time was seven for rehearsal. It was "tech week"—crunch time for the cast and crew. The next week, there would be a dress rehearsal, followed by a Friday night opening. Monica and Ben had secured seats in a private box for Saturday evening, the night after the opening of the show. They didn't want anything to possibly ruin opening night, so they purposely planned to stay away.

Ben had hired a highly recommended bodyguard for Saturday night, hoping to pretend to be a normal family spending an evening together, even if only for a few hours. They had low expectations of that materializing, however. They had had little experience over the years with being a normal family. It was one of the biggest drawbacks of working in "the business."

Normally Juliette might have poured the family some glasses of Chianti to go with the meal. She had mentioned to Ben and Monica earlier that she didn't believe that to be a good idea, and they agreed. They were determined to do whatever it would take for Brent to get better, even if that meant they wouldn't touch another drop of alcohol the rest of their lives.

The family was quiet when they first sat down at the table, but then Brent asked about the play, and the tension in the air slowly began to dissipate. Bart launched into an excited description of the story's plot and the top-notch acting company. Later, Ben told them about the movie he had just completed in Asia, with a play-by-play of the behavior of a slightly eccentric director.

By the time the brownies and ice cream were served, they even found themselves laughing. Juliette smiled widely as she began to take the dishes back to the kitchen. She hadn't heard laughter inside this house in years. It was such a delightful sound.

After dessert and coffee, Bart had to go. He hated to leave, but he had no choice. The twin brothers rose in tandem, which they so often did on so many things. Brent walked Bart to the door.

"Break a leg, bro," Brent said softly as they reached the entryway, then hugged his brother like he was hanging on for dear life.

Bart looked at him with misty eyes. "It's going to be okay. I don't know how, but it's going to be okay," he said, firmly gripping his brother's shoulder.

Brent just nodded at his twin, hoping with all of his heart that he was right.

Marty arrived back at school mid-afternoon. She dropped off her backpack at her place and immediately went to Michael's efficiency down the hall. She stood outside the door for a moment, took a deep breath, and knocked on the door. There was no answer, so she knocked harder. Finally, she heard footsteps approaching.

The door slowly opened, and there was Michael's surprised face in front of her. "Marty!" he exclaimed. He pulled her to himself and held her tightly. He wanted to kiss her, but considering their unhappy parting a few days earlier, he wasn't sure she would want him to.

He gently released her. "Come on in," he said, and they stepped into the messy room. Exam time had a way of destroying a small space. Michael had also been beside himself the past few days, and that didn't lend itself to picking up either.

Michael looked at Marty, and Marty looked at Michael. Then they both began to speak at the same time.

"I think we should go to Africa," Michael blurted out.

"I think we should go to Peru," Marty said simultaneously.

"What?" They both said at the same time.

"Okay, this is ridiculous. You go first, Michael," Marty suggested.

"I want to go to Africa. Wherever you want to be, I want to be," he said sincerely.

"I want to go to Peru," she replied.

Michael looked at her in disbelief. "Peru? I thought you always dreamed of living and working in Africa?"

"I did, but there are good people in Peru, too. And the Zika virus—it is very important to get a handle on it as soon as possible. It will be groundbreaking work," she said, with real excitement in her voice.

He searched her face. "Are you sure? A few days ago..."

"A lot can happen in a few days. A person can discover that there is nowhere on earth that is more important than being with someone you love," she said, admitting for the first time that she loved him.

Michael looked happily surprised. "You love me?" he asked.

"I do. I love you, Michael," Marty said, tears shining in her eyes.

"That's good, because I love you, too, Marty. So much," he said, and pulled her into an embrace.

That evening, Marty and Michael sat next to each other on the couch, their laptops sitting on theirs knees. On the count of three, they simultaneously accepted their residencies in Lima. They toasted their new positions with mugs of coffee, as there was still a lot of studying to be done before the night was over. Afterward, they called their families to give them the news of their decisions.

John and Jillian watched Marty's face over the video call in amazement. Just days before, she had come home disillusioned and heartbroken. Now, she looked happy and excited.

"What changed your mind?" John asked.

"A couple of things. One, I was miserable away from Michael

for just a few days, so I would expect that a few years apart would not be a very good option. And breaking up—that would be the worst thing ever. Two, meeting Luz. It helped me wake up to the fact that there are wonderful people everywhere in the world, not just in Africa. The people in South America are just as important, and the health issues are just as urgent there as they are elsewhere. It took meeting someone from another continent to help me see that. I'm so glad that Luz came to dinner at our house," she said sincerely.

John and Jillian nodded their heads in agreement. They talked a few more minutes, then Marty had to get back to studying for her exam the next morning. It was a three-hour exam, with two ten-minute breaks. That would be nothing compared to the final boards, however. That would be the next hurdle before they left for their residencies. The next month would be consumed with studying. The only break would be for one special day—the day of Marty's formal adoption.

The night of the dinner at John and Jillian's, Carson Stone had dropped off Luz at her rented condo at ten-thirty p.m. It had been a fairly quiet ride home, the usually verbose Carson again at a loss for words, as he had been on and off throughout the evening whenever he was close to Luz. He didn't know why he felt so strange around this woman. Part of it could be that he thought she was the most beautiful person he had ever met—inside and out. He had known she was physically stunning, but he had loved watching her talk to John and Jillian's daughter that evening, telling Marty about her home country, and being so kind and encouraging to the young woman who was facing a tough life choice.

He stopped the car, jumped out of his Model X Tesla, and went around to the passenger door to open it for Luz. She seemed surprised by this gesture, but smiled at him as he helped her out of the luxurious seat. She stood up, her eyes meeting his, as they were about the same height with Luz wearing flats on this occasion. His eyes were kind eyes, she thought. Carson Stone had been a nice surprise. She had heard that he could be a difficult person to work with, but she hadn't encountered anything of the sort—at least not yet.

Being face-to-face—and so close—made Carson suddenly back away. He felt extremely self-conscious. He knew he was not a handsome man by most people's standards, and Luz—she was an otherworldly beauty. He suddenly wished he was taller and good-looking, like John Romano. Instead, he felt small, weak, and inadequate.

"Good night, Luz," he finally croaked out.

"Thank you for the ride home, Mr. Stone," Luz said.

"Call me Carson—please," he told her.

"Thank you for the ride home—Carson," she said, with a smile that made his heart jump. "I will see you in the morning," she added over her shoulder as she walked toward the door of her unit, only a few steps away.

"Yes, bright and early. Sleep well," he said, and climbed back into the car. He waited until she got the door unlocked, then she waved to him, and he waved back. He watched the door close and stared at it for a few seconds afterward. *What a special person you are, Luz,* he thought, as he quietly drove away.

Jillian was amazed how quickly things in life could change. She felt upbeat as she and John drove into the studio that morning. She had decided to go early again to write while he was in make-up, finding that arrangement to be quite advantageous. She was almost halfway through the first draft of the book she was writing to help those who had lost babies or experienced complications with pregnancies or childbirth.

Two days earlier, she had dreaded watching John and Luz work together. Now she felt comfortable with the situation. Two days before, her daughter wanted to live and work in Africa. Now she had accepted a position in Lima, Peru. Jillian gave part of the credit for that decision to Luz. Funny how one's opinion of another person could flip-flop so quickly as well.

That thought made Jillian think about Monica. She needed to touch base with her again, soon. She was very thankful that Ben was now back, so they could support each other and their son during this time. She also needed to call Greta and set up a time to get together and talk about the world of new motherhood. The poor woman had looked beside herself when she and John had left the other day. That, and completely exhausted.

Jillian made notes in her phone of the numerous calls that she needed to make. It was a pretty lengthy list. She thanked God for that as she typed in the names. Only sixteen months ago, she had come to Los Angeles knowing no one. Now, her life was filled with many special friends, and she was a married woman.

She was shaking her head at the thought when Luz came out of makeup and stopped to talk. Jillian was happy to see her and tell her the news about Marty and Michael.

"Thank you so much for all your help, Luz," Jillian said. "You made a huge impression on our daughter. She said that now she knows that there are wonderful people everywhere, and that comment was based on her meeting you."

Even with all the makeup and her darker complexion, Jillian could see a hint of a blush in Luz' face.

"Thank you for such a special compliment. I was equally impressed with Marty. You must be so proud."

"We are," she answered smiling.

Luz looked thoughtful for a moment. "It was a wonderful evening..." She didn't finish her sentence. She looked around. "What do you know about Carson Stone?" Luz asked quietly.

Jillian wondered if something had happened on the way home for such a question to arise. She told her the few things she knew—about her experiences in Alaska and how she came to be involved in this movie because of them.

Then Luz looked around once more. "Is he...married?"

"No, I don't believe so," she said.

Just then John joined them, and the subject was dropped. It was time for everyone to get to work. Jillian made a mental note to find out more about Carson Stone later that night. Luz' curiosity had piqued her own. Jillian was getting pretty good at doing research on her computer, so later, she would see what she could learn about this intriguing man. She added "research CS" to her to-do list on her phone before she got too busy to remember.

Work went well that day, although Jillian thought that Carson had acted a bit strange. She wondered again if something had happened on the ride home the other night. As soon as she put the last of the dishes in the dishwasher, she pulled out her laptop. John had gone to feed and brush Lucy and start some laundry, so it was a perfect time to do a little bit of research.

She found the familiar celebrity biographies. One mentioned that he was born "Steven Carson," in Beulah, North Dakota. Next, she Googled Steven Carson, but found no news about anyone by that name. She decided to look for articles in the *Beulah Beacon,* the town's local newspaper. He was bound to have been an honor student in high school, or maybe he played a sport, although he did not appear to be an athletic type. She was certain that his name would show up somewhere. One would think he would be

Kathy J. Jacobson

the toast of the town having become so successful.

She had almost given up, when she caught a very brief mention of the Carson name in the "social page" from 1978. In it was an apology from the Smith and Carson families. It mentioned that anyone who had given a wedding gift or card to "Steve and Cindy" could retrieve them at the Methodist Church in town until the end of the month. After that time, any remaining items or money would be donated to charity.

While it didn't give any details, Jillian was quite sure that "Steve" was Carson Stone. He had been planning to get married, and something happened. From the sadness she had seen in his eyes a few days before, and the comments he had made about how lucky she was to be able to trust John, she imagined that Carson had not been the one to call off the wedding.

She looked at the social column in the next few months' editions. There was a mention three months later that "that poor boy who was left at the altar" was moving to California. It didn't say his name, but Jillian was sure everyone knew who "that poor boy" was. No wonder Carson had changed his name, and no wonder, as he had told them the other night at dinner, that he hadn't been back to his hometown since he was nineteen. It was one thing to be jilted on your wedding day. It was in the category of "horrific" to have it be everybody's business.

Jillian felt terrible for Carson. She knew what it felt like to be rejected. She knew the feeling of embarrassment, too, although she thought Carson's situation took the prize in the humiliation department. She said a prayer for him. She prayed that he would learn to love and trust again—and that that person would be worthy of his love and trust.

Jillian knew it would be no easy task. She herself had run away from her own feelings. But she also knew now that one could love again, and one could trust again—if one found the right person.

Her eyes moved to her wedding ring, and she fingered the band, the one with the words "the right person" engraved on the inside.

Just then John came back into the room. She closed the laptop, and her eyes filled with incredible love for him as she watched him walk toward her. Her own prayers had been answered, more completely and incredibly than she ever thought possible. A smile swept across her face, and he returned it with that special grin. *Thank you, Lord.*

The next morning, Jillian and Luz made small talk while they waited for John to come out of makeup. They both found it humorous that it took him longer than it did Luz. When they made a comment about it to John when he emerged, he told them it took longer for him because they had a lot more work to do to make him look reasonably decent next to someone like Luz. Jillian knew she was "over the hump" of feeling uncomfortable with the John-Luz situation when she could laugh and joke right along with words like that.

She didn't feel that she could share any of the information she had learned about Carson the night before. For one thing, she had not verified that he was indeed the person in the articles. Also, she hoped that perhaps she would get a chance to talk to him sometime. If, and when, a good time presented itself, she would ask him. It wasn't the kind of thing someone would just bring up out of the blue. She would know if there was a right time.

Jillian had seen Carson get frustrated, even angry, on the set before. Usually, it happened when things went wrong, like Chase Cheekwood dislocating his finger during a fight scene, or an actor named Jones leaking photos to the tabloids when they were

Kathy J. Jacobson

filming in Alaska. But she had never seen him be mean to an actor for no apparent reason. What started as coolness early in the day, grew into blatant putdowns by the end of it. Every little line, every little movement that Luz said or did was ripped apart by Carson, often in very derogatory ways.

Jillian began to think that perhaps something bad had happened the night Carson gave Luz a ride home. Maybe Carson had asked Luz out, and she rejected him. Maybe that was why Luz was asking her earlier if he was married. Maybe she wanted more information before she said "yes" to an invitation. She didn't know what it was, she only knew something was very wrong, and needed to change—fast.

John had an appointment with Buck at the end of the workday, giving the rancher a tour of the Esperanza Workshop. John had flashed a concerned look at Jillian before he left. She was pretty sure he was suggesting that she say something to Carson about his negative behavior. She was getting pretty good at reading John. John would probably have said something to her, had Carson not been standing just feet away from them when they said goodbye.

Jillian noticed Luz hurrying to her dressing room at the end of the shoot, looking like she might burst into tears at any moment. Jillian felt she had to say something to Carson, one way or the other. If she was truly considered one of the assistants on the production, she thought that she had the right to do so—for the sake of the movie, if not for the sake of her friends.

She hugged John and then followed Carson. He didn't know that Jillian was right behind him, and when he got near a locker at the end of the hallway, he kicked it angrily. It was a good thing he was wearing boots, or he might have broken a bone. He reached down to grab his sore foot and let out an expletive, another thing Jillian had never heard him do. Something was definitely not right.

She stood and watched for a moment, until he noticed her

standing there.

"Jillian. I'm...sorry...I'm..." Carson was at a loss for words, another rarity.

"Carson, let's go somewhere and talk," she suggested.

He hesitated. "All right. We do need to go over some notes for tomorrow," he said.

"We do," Jillian agreed gently. "But we also need to go over today."

His complexion turned crimson, and he simply nodded. "My office. Ten minutes," he said.

Jillian nodded in response.

Carson was standing and looking out the window directly behind his desk. Jillian had been shown in by his secretary, who announced her arrival. He continued to stare out the window even after she entered. Jillian wasn't quite sure how to proceed, so she just took a seat on the soft, leather couch and waited for him to make the next move.

Finally, he turned around and faced her. His face looked ashen, and his eyes were red and watery.

"I'm sorry about today," he said after a moment.

"I don't think I'm the one who needs to hear an apology, Carson," Jillian said.

"I don't imagine that Luz would want to hear *anything* from someone like me, ever again."

The way he said this sentence made Jillian hurt for both of her friends.

"I think you might be surprised," Jillian said. She paused, then asked, "Did something happen after dinner at our house the other night?"

He plopped down into his desk chair.

Kathy J. Jacobson

"Why do you ask?"

"Because yesterday, you seemed different. And today—well, to-day—that was something else, to say the least," she said honestly.

"I got a bit testy," he answered, suddenly a bit defensive and trying to downplay his behavior.

"I don't know many actors who would be as gracious as Luz was today, when treated like she was by you," Jillian said. "If she didn't like you and respect you as much as she does..."

Carson cut Jillian off in a gruff voice. "Who says she likes me?"

"I can tell that she likes you." Jillian said.

"I don't want her to like me, and I don't want to like..." He stopped his sentence short.

Jillian wasn't sure if this was the right time or not, but she decided to go for it.

"It's okay to like someone, Carson," she said.

"No, it's not! Not for me, anyway," he retorted. "You don't understand what..." His voice trailed off.

"I understand more than you think I do," she answered. Carson's eyebrows raised in surprise. "And even if I don't know *your* entire story, I know *mine*." She proceeded to relay the story of Dr. Jeffrey Lawrence, Marty's biological father, and then her heartbreak with Pastor Scott Bradford. Afterward she told him how she met John and came within minutes of leaving him for good. "I almost missed the love of my life by attempting to run away. If that taxi had arrived five minutes earlier, I wouldn't be married to John and I wouldn't be sitting here today."

"But that's you, and not me," he said. "I'm not someone anyone would want to marry."

His words stabbed at her heart again. "I don't believe that, Carson," she replied.

"If you only knew...," he said, looking distant.

"What—if I knew that once you were terribly hurt?"

His head snapped to attention. He searched her face. "What do you think you know?" he asked quietly.

"Were you once Steven Carson?"

"I was, but I haven't gone by that name since I was nineteen, when I moved here after..." He stopped speaking.

"After you were hurt by someone you loved?" she asked gently.

"How did you find that out?" He paused. "It doesn't really matter, does it?"

"It does if it is still causing you this much pain this many years later. And it does if it is keeping you from ever letting anyone into your heart again," she said.

Carson was quiet for a minute, then spoke. "We were going to move here right after the wedding. I was nineteen. Cindy was eighteen and had just graduated from high school. I waited for her for an entire year. I worked two jobs and saved enough money for both of us to leave and follow our dreams for the future.

"She left me waiting at the church and ran off with Billy, a handsome, tall basketball player who promised her a great life in Bismarck. He had a job already as a supermarket manager. I think he's still the manager at the same store. Her mother had told her that I would be a flop in Hollywood, and of course, she believed her. And there was no way I could compete in the looks department with someone like Billy." He paused again. "She didn't even tell me in person. She had her friend give me a note! If I wasn't good enough for a girl from Beulah, how in the world could I possibly be good enough..." He didn't finish his sentence, but he didn't have to.

After considering his words, Jillian spoke. "You know, Carson, Luz has been judged almost her entire life purely by her looks. Did you ever think that perhaps she feels the same way about love that you do, except she thinks people only want her because of her beauty and because she is famous? You two might have a lot more in common than you think. I also feel she deserves more credit than you are giving her."

Carson was quiet. He appeared to be mulling over Jillian's words.

"Did you really want to go over notes for tomorrow, or should we call it a day?" she asked.

"I think this day needs to be called," he answered seriously.

"Carson, you're a good man—don't forget that. I wouldn't be working with you if you weren't. Good night," she said, standing up.

He stood up, looking spent. "Good night...and thank you, Jillian."

She gave him a reassuring smile as she walked toward the door, inwardly saying a prayer for the healing of yet another broken heart.

Chapter Nine

B uck sauntered toward the Esperanza Workshop, wearing his cowboy boots and favorite off-white suit and hat combination. He was an unusual sight in the neighborhood. Western wear was far from the norm in this particular area.

He walked past the buildings that were riddled with graffiti and broken windows. He did not have a smart phone, so he pulled out a piece of paper to check the address again when he heard someone speaking to him.

"Stick 'em up, cowboy!" a young, angry voice said.

He turned around and faced a young black man, who had his hand in the pocket of a torn vest, pointing a supposed gun at Buck.

Buck stood six inches taller than the man, and with his hat, he seemed even bigger.

"Not a good idea, young man," Buck answered calmly.

"I want your wallet and your watch, and nobody will get hurt," the man said.

"And I want you to turn around and start walking the other direction, son, and nobody will get hurt," Buck said back to him.

"I'm not your son, old man," he retorted and started to pull his hand out of his pocket.

Buck grabbed his arm. He was right in assuming the man had no real gun. They grappled for a few moments. The younger man was wild with fear and anger, and landed one good punch to Buck's face, which sent him to the ground. But that only made Buck angrier, and he grabbed the man's leg and pulled him down to the sidewalk beside him. Within moments, he had him face down on the cement with his arms behind his back.

Meanwhile, someone going into the Esperanza Workshop had called 9-1-1, and told John there was a crime going on outside. John ran outside to see if he could help, and was horrified when he saw Buck on the ground. He ran to his side, just as the police arrived at the scene.

The officers grabbed the young man, read him his rights, and put him in handcuffs. Buck looked him in the eye before the officer put his hand on his head to protect him as he was guided into the back seat of the police car.

"I told you to walk away," he said to the young man.

The officer asked him for a statement. Buck told him exactly what had happened, then asked what was going to happened to the "kid."

"He'll probably be locked up for a while. It's not his first time, and assault isn't going to look good to the judge," the officer said.

"Isn't there some other way to handle this?" Buck asked.

"Like what?" the officer asked.

"Like—he could work it off?"

"I don't think there's any way. It will be up to the judge tomorrow morning."

Buck asked for the details about the court proceeding. The officer looked at him like he was from another planet, but answered his questions politely.

After the squad car pulled away from the curb, John put his

hand on Buck's shoulder, a concerned look on his face. The officer had given Buck an ice pack for his face, which Buck held against his cheekbone.

"Are you okay, Buck? I'm so sorry that this happened," John said in an apologetic tone.

"Oh, it's just kids being stupid. I was a stupid kid once, so I know about these things. Anyway, let's see this place of yours," he said, putting the pack in his pocket and dusting off his hat nonchalantly with this hand.

They walked down the block to the only building around that wasn't a wreck, the Esperanza Workshop site. John spent the next hour showing Buck the facility and introducing him to Bobbi and Brooks and some of the young people in the acting class. They were all very respectful to Buck. Part of that was because word had already gotten around that he had just taken down one of the troublemakers in the "hood," right outside of the Workshop. It appeared to impress them.

Buck was equally impressed with what he saw and heard at the Esperanza Workshop.

"Y'alls doing good things here, John," he said.

"I'm glad you think so, Buck. We feel like it is making a difference, even if in only small ways—to begin with," he said smiling, although he still felt terrible about what had happened to Buck just a half-block away.

"Y'alls are, and God bless y'alls for it," Buck said sincerely, as he put his hat back on to leave the building.

John walked with Buck to his truck to see him off safely, then walked quickly to his car on the next block. It was an intimidating place once the sun began to set. He hoped that one day the Workshop would expand to help more people in more ways, and it would help change the climate of the neighborhood. That was his prayer as he drove home.

Kathy J. Jacobson

Greta's cell phone rang. She recognized the number, and her heart began to pound. It was the head of the search committee at the small university to which she had applied—her top choice. She nervously fumbled for her phone and answered.

"Hello, this is Greta Alexander," she said.

"Ms. Alexander, I hope I'm not interrupting your dinner," a bright voice said.

"No, you are not," she said. She didn't really have much of an appetite these days. She would have some leftovers with Drew when he arrived home.

"We would like to offer you the position of assistant professor, if you are still interested," the woman continued.

"I am interested, and will gladly accept," she said. It was her dream job. She didn't need any time to think about this one.

"I am so very glad to hear that," the woman replied. "We were very impressed with your portfolio, as well as your philosophy and vision for the art department."

Greta was thrilled, but thought to herself, *you won't be very happy to hear that I'm pregnant when I can't hide it anymore.*

They set up a time to meet early the next week. Greta hoped that it would be in the afternoon, when she felt better, and was thrilled when the woman gave her options of times, including a 3:00 p.m. meeting on Tuesday. They would send her a contract to look over. She could sign it on Tuesday, and negotiate any changes with them before that time.

Greta hung up just as Drew walked into the house. She ran to him, the most excited she had been in weeks.

"We should go out and celebrate!" he said, so happy to see Greta cheerful. She had been so tired and down lately, so unlike herself.

After Greta decided on a type of food that sounded at least

somewhat appealing, they made a reservation and arrived right on the dot. The waiter brought a bottle of wine to the table and asked if they would like to try it. Greta wanted to toast with a glass so badly, but couldn't. She could feel the resentment growing inside of her, as she mentioned that she would have to decline. Drew was kind enough to pass on it, too, which was helpful. They ordered a non-alcoholic drink called a "Baby Bellini," made with peach concentrate and fresh raspberries. It was tasty, refreshing, and colorful, and was served in champagne glasses, which made it feel celebratory.

Greta spoke excitedly about her new position as they shared a simple appetizer. She thought the school was up-and-coming and the art department was gaining a good reputation. She and the dean of the department meshed well on many levels, too. Drew hadn't seen Greta this animated in a long time, and he couldn't stop smiling as he listened to her. He reached across the table and held her hand as she continued.

"They are hoping I would be willing to take students abroad eventually. I did a trip like that between my sophomore and junior years. I would love to go back to some of those places in Europe again," she said, her fiery green eyes blazing with excitement.

They ordered the crab melt dinner and the quinoa with roasted red peppers and tofu, sharing the dishes, along with a "farmer's salad," which was almost a meal in itself. Greta enjoyed her meal for the first time in weeks. She surprised herself with how much food she had eaten. Even more surprising, however, was that she found herself smiling—even laughing—from time to time, throughout the evening.

As they drove home, Greta felt optimistic about the future, and better physically than she had in a long time. Unfortunately, the feeling wouldn't last long.

That night, Greta was awakened from a deep sleep by an intense pain in her lower back. She tried to think if she had lifted something the day before, or done any unusual exercise, but couldn't recall anything out of the ordinary. She sat up in bed, then suddenly felt like she needed to use the restroom.

She hurried to the bathroom, and another spasm hit her in the back and the abdomen. She had the oddest feeling and hoped that she didn't have food poisoning. Drew had eaten the same foods she had, though, and he was sleeping soundly, so she didn't think it was that. Then she saw the bright red and brown flowage and let out a gasp.

Drew drove Greta to the hospital. By the time they arrived, she had lost a lot of blood and clots of tissue. Even though they hadn't seen a doctor yet, Greta knew in her mind, and felt in her heart, that she was no longer pregnant.

Drew's eyes were red, but Greta sat like a stone when the doctor confirmed a miscarriage. The doctor was saying something about not needing any additional treatment, but Greta didn't really hear what she said. At the end, the doctor handed her a sheet with discharge instructions, then gave them some pamphlets about what to expect after a miscarriage, both physically and emotionally. Another one was for a support group of some type.

Drew and Greta were silent on the way home. Greta stared out the window of the vehicle, still in a daze. As they neared their home, Drew began to say something about not going in to work, but Greta cut him off.

"That's not necessary, Drew. I will be fine," she lied.

"I could come home early after the meeting," he said.

"No rush, really. I'm okay," she insisted. All she wanted was to be alone.

"I will just go to the meeting and be home right after that," he said, as they entered the house.

He reached for her and pulled her into an embrace.

"I'm so sorry, honey," he said, and kissed her forehead.

She nodded. Tears filled her eyes as he held her. Then Drew showered, got dressed, and reluctantly left for work.

Greta watched Drew drive away. As his vehicle turned the corner and was out of sight, she began to cry softly, then to sob violently. She had never felt emptier in her entire life. She had never felt like such a horrible person in her entire life. She hadn't wanted to be pregnant, and now she wasn't. *This is all your fault. You didn't want to be a mother—not yet, anyway. You don't deserve to be one.* That is what she told herself.

She went to the bedroom, pulled the blinds, and slipped back into bed. She stayed there until Drew got home from his meeting in the mid-afternoon. The only exceptions were several trips to the bathroom. She didn't want food. She didn't want to talk to anyone. She just wanted to drop off the face of the planet.

Drew did everything he could to try to be helpful, but the more kindness he exhibited, the worse it made Greta feel inside. He had called both sets of parents to tell them the news. They were sad and disappointed, but mostly concerned about Drew and especially about Greta. They offered to come over, but Greta adamantly refused their help, saying that she wasn't up to having company yet. She wouldn't even speak for more than a moment to her own mother, with whom she was usually quite close.

Drew had also called Jillian. He had overheard her telling Greta she would call her sometime soon, and he didn't want her to call and be surprised by such terrible news. Jillian had been driving on the freeway when Drew called, so their conversation was brief. Jillian extended her sympathies and told him that either one of them could call her anytime to talk, and to let her know if there was anything else she could do. He thanked her and told her he would keep her in the loop.

On the way to church Sunday morning, Jillian and John remarked about the past week. It had been full of incredible ups and downs. First, there was the Marty and Michael situation. It had started out looking so bleak, but made a huge turnaround mid-week.

Then there was the situation between Carson and Luz. After a wonderful evening at John and Jillian's home on Monday evening, Carson had turned into a person they didn't recognize as the week progressed. Once Jillian had confirmed the facts of his past with Carson, she told John the little she knew. She thought that Carson was falling in love with Luz and was very frightened, causing him to behave so poorly. At least by Friday, his behavior had improved somewhat. He was cooler than usual toward everyone, but at least the hypercriticism of Luz had subsided.

Then Buck had gone down to the Workshop to take a tour and was almost mugged. He was all right, but John still felt awful about the situation.

Lastly, there was the news about Drew and Greta. Only the weekend before they had made their big announcement, which had turned into heartbreak by the end of the week. Drew had also mentioned on his call to Jillian that Greta had gotten her dream job, but that wonderful news was greatly overshadowed by the loss of the baby.

Jillian had anonymously written about Drew and Greta's situation online, as pregnancy loss was the main subject of her current book, and her blog at present. This close-to-home loss certainly made her project seem even more important—and personal— than before, and she found her eyes filling with tears as she typed in the news. She would give Greta some time to grieve, but would be sure to touch base with her soon, once the shock of the event wore off.

As Jillian sat down in the pew at church, she prayed for her family and friends and the events of the past week. Midway through her inward litany, John took her hand. She thought she could feel his prayers being lifted up simultaneously, as his fingers wrapped tightly around hers, his eyes closed, and head bowed. She tacked on another prayer of thanks as she finished—for her partner in prayer, and in life.

John and Jillian had been sitting near the front of the sanctuary, so when they turned to leave, they were in for a surprise—actually, a couple of them.

First, they were greeted by the smiling faces of Karen, Robert, and Rick, who were just coming out of a pew in the back. Rick, apparently, had gone to Sunday School before the service so they came in at the last minute. The pastor's twin sons had been sitting with them, wanting to be by Rick, whom they idolized. Jillian had originally thought that perhaps the twins had spent the night at their grandparents' home when she had noticed Pastor Jim's wife, Janet, sitting near the front by herself.

The biggest surprise, however, was the sight of Buck, Nancy, and their "guest." John almost didn't recognize the young man at first. It was Buck's assailant from the street a few days before, whose name they learned was Darius. The young man's gaze never left the floor, and he looked like he would rather be anywhere other than where he was. The exception may have been a jail cell, which was his only other alternative.

Apparently, Buck had told the judge that Darius could work off his offense at the ranch. The judge was very skeptical, but gave it a six-week trial. After that point, they would come back to court, and he would make a more informed decision.

John and Jillian offered to host lunch and swimming at their house. Buck said they had work to do at the ranch, but certainly another time. Pastor Jim, Janet, and their boys, Karen, Robert, and

Rick all said they would be over shortly. On the way home, Jillian called for groceries, and John called and invited Pete and Kelly over, too. It had been way too long since they had seen the couple and their adorable, changing-by-the-minute babies.

At home on the ranch, Nancy cooked a chicken dinner while Buck and Darius went to feed the horses. Darius was very hesitant near the huge animals, and Buck could tell he was frightened. He patiently showed him what to do, giving him simple jobs to do at first, not requiring him to get too close. It would take time for someone from the city to adjust to the farm. Buck knew how that felt. While he hadn't lived in a city like Los Angeles, he had been a "town kid" until he was fifteen. That was the year his life had changed.

Buck and Darius washed their hands in the mudroom of the huge, two-story ranch house, then went to sit down at the large oval, oak table in the dining room. Buck helped Nancy put the chicken, biscuits, and vegetables in the center of the table. Buck could tell that Darius was hungry and liked the looks of his meal, but he was trying his hardest not to show it.

It was a quiet dinner, with Buck and Nancy doing almost all of the conversing. They talked about church that morning. Nancy asked Darius if he attended a church. He said he had gone when he was a little boy, with his grandmother. He said she always went to services and was always reading her Bible. But then he tacked on angrily, "A lot of good it did her. She got shot in a drive-by."

"Oh, my goodness," Nancy said. "I'm so sorry, Darius."

He didn't answer and pushed his plate away. At least he was almost done with his food by that time.

Nancy was at a loss for words. She waited for a moment, then asked if they wanted dessert, not knowing what else to say.

"How about some pie and ice cream?" she asked.

Darius just sat there, not answering.

"How about when we come back in from our chores this afternoon?" Buck asked, putting his hand on Nancy's reassuringly.

"Thank you for the wonderful meal, darlin'," he said to her, as he got up. He hugged her on the way to his hat.

"Thank you," Darius said quietly, and stood as well.

"You are both welcome," she said. She looked kindly at Darius as he left the room, but wondered if, and how, they would be able to help him. She looked up to heaven and lifted a prayer for this hurt and troubled young soul.

Buck and Darius' next project was digging holes for fence posts. They were alone on this one, as Buck's two hired hands were busy feeding the cattle and chickens and his weekend foreman had the afternoon off for a family event. The two hired hands lived in two cottages on the ranch property, each with his wife and children. His weekday and weekend foremen owned their own homes not far away.

The soil was hard because of the lack of rain, and Darius was tiring quickly. He was not accustomed to so much physical work, and post-digging is never an enjoyable job under any circumstance. When Buck thought he had had enough, he suggested they take a break and have some water that he had brought with him in a jug. They sat on the ground, another thing that Buck could tell was new to Darius. Buck noticed him squirm away from an insect. Buck looked away, as not to embarrass him. Buck remembered the first time he had seen a mouse in a barn. He had let out quite a shriek.

After ten minutes, they were back at it. It was hard work, but Darius had a naturally athletic body. Buck could see that the young man was proud when Buck mentioned how strong he was,

Kathy J. Jacobson

and promised him that he would be even stronger in six weeks. They worked another hour, then headed back to the house.

"Does that pie and ice cream sound good now?" Buck asked as they approached the home.

Darius just nodded, but Buck knew he was looking forward to it.

Nancy was reading in the three-seasons room when they came back. Buck stuck his head into the room and asked if it was okay if they had some dessert now. He told her that they could serve themselves, unless she wanted to join them.

Nancy decided that the more time Darius could spend getting to know Buck, the better. So she told them she was still too full from Sunday dinner, "unlike you men who just worked for three hours digging in the dirt."

Darius was on his second helping of apple pie and ice cream when Buck told him what the next day's schedule would be like. Darius' eyes were huge when Buck told him the work day would begin at 5:00 a.m., with breakfast before that if he wanted it.

"And you're going to want it. All this physical work makes a man hungry," he said, smiling at Darius, who was practically licking the plate the pie had been on. There was a hint of a smile at the corners of Darius' mouth, but Buck could tell he was stubborn and wouldn't let his emotions show, just like Buck had once been.

Buck picked up his plate and utensils, took them to the sink and rinsed them before putting them in the dishwasher. Darius watched Buck closely, then followed behind him with his plate and silverware and did the same. Buck went back to the table with a damp dishcloth and wiped the table clean.

"I'm going to get cleaned up before supper. We don't do a big meal on Sunday nights, usually. Just something light. I hope that's okay with you," he said.

"You mean we get to eat again?" Darius asked, surprised. Then he looked embarrassed.

"Yes, we are very blessed in this household," Buck said sincerely. "Y'all is welcome to do whatever you please until dinner at seven o'clock. There's a television in the family room, books in the library, or the porch for sitting. Or hit the shower—that's another option, too. It's your call, Darius."

Buck could tell that Darius had no clue what to do with himself, but he quietly walked up the stairs to his room, which had a small bathroom with his own shower. Buck was also pretty sure that Darius had never had such luxurious living accommodations in his entire life. The young man's head must have been spinning with all the new things that were happening in his world.

Buck watched him as he reached the top step, and as Nancy had earlier, said a silent prayer for God's help and guidance—for Darius and for himself.

Chapter Ten

Drew kissed Greta and regretfully said goodbye Monday morning. She was still in bed, unusual for the woman who loved the freshness of the early hours, often remarking about how good the light was for an art project of some sort.

She had been subdued all weekend, and nothing Drew did or said seemed to help. In fact, he thought that perhaps his efforts were making it worse. He had read some of the pamphlets the doctor had given them after Greta had gone to bed early last night—again, not her usual pattern. He was searching for answers. He had gone online afterward, looking for more information. He knew it was all still very fresh, but from what he was reading, and just his sense about his wife, he thought something was very wrong. He decided that if he had a chance today, he was going to call Jillian again. She used to be a nurse. Perhaps she would have some suggestions.

A little after ten o'clock, Greta forced herself to get out of bed. She dragged herself into the bathroom and made herself step into the shower. As the hot, steamy water streamed over her face, tears flowed along with it. She felt like crying all the time, and now that

Drew wasn't around, she could let herself go.

She tried to focus her mind on her meeting the next afternoon at the university. At least she didn't have to worry about explaining a pregnancy to them, but her relief about that fact made guilt rage within her, causing her to cry even harder.

After Greta toweled herself dry and dressed, she sat at the kitchen table, a cup of coffee in her hands. She didn't think anything of it at first, but she was drinking coffee for the first time in six weeks. While she was pregnant, just the smell of it made her wretch. She looked at the pottery mug in her hands—one of her favorites of her own creations—then abruptly stood up and violently threw it toward the sink. It hit the counter in front of the basin, shattering into pieces and splattering its steaming contents everywhere. Greta felt just like her broken mug as she sat down and sobbed into her folded arms on the table. After a few minutes she lifted her head and looked at the wreckage. *You need help.*

Jillian hit the contact number for Greta. Drew had called and left a message for her that morning on his way to work, and she had called him back during one of her breaks. His report had not sounded very hopeful. She had never heard Drew talk like he had that morning. His obvious love for Greta, and his intuition about her, were truly amazing to Jillian. If he had been even a fraction that attentive to Jillian when they had dated, their relationship may have been a "go."

Greta dried her eyes with a napkin and stood up to attend to the mess she had made, when her cell phone chimed. She wasn't going to answer it, until she saw Jillian's name flash across the screen. She took a deep breath, hit the accept button, and timidly said hello.

It was difficult to hear the voice on the end of the line, and Jillian wasn't sure she had the right person. Could this be the confident, almost fierce at times Greta that she knew? It sounded like someone doing a weak imitation of her.

"Is this Greta?" Jillian asked.

"It's me, Jillian," Greta replied.

"I was just thinking about you and wondering what you were doing this evening? Would you like to get together—at your house or mine, or somewhere else?" Jillian asked.

"How about your house? I need to get out of here," Greta said, sounding desperate.

Jillian wished she was free right away, but it just wasn't possible. "I'll be home by six at the latest. Give me a time," she said.

They settled on seven o'clock. John was scheduled for some night filming, which did not require her attendance. It would be perfect. Jillian invited Greta to eat with her, but Greta said another time, that Jillian should go ahead and eat before she got there. Jillian was even more concerned after their conversation than she had been before, and was very happy that Greta had agreed to come over. She sounded like someone who needed help—badly.

John noticed Jillian's concerned look when she came back from making her call. He walked up to her, putting his hand on her arm.

"Not good?" he asked. He knew that she had been talking to Greta.

Jillian was going to say something just as Carson called them back to their places. She simply shook her head "no," and told him quickly that Greta was coming over at seven.

"If anyone can help her, it will be you," he said, kindly and confidently, giving her arm a squeeze. Then it was time to get back to work.

The next scene was between John and Luz. At the end of it, John was supposed to kiss her passionately. Jillian thought the scene had gone quite nicely, but Carson disagreed. He had them do it a second time. Then a third. Jillian began to wonder if Carson was doing this on purpose, to get back at her for digging into his past.

When he called for them to do it for a fourth time, Jillian thought about leaving the room. It wasn't that it was bothering her—she was getting fairly used to this type of thing—but she could tell that John and Luz were getting frustrated, and she thought their kisses looked less and less authentic as they continued on.

Finally, on the fifth take, Carson lost it.

"For God's sake, man, kiss the woman!" he said, getting up hastily from his director's chair.

He stomped over to the two of them.

"You've got the most beautiful woman in the world in front of you, and you kiss her like that."

"So, how would you like me to kiss her?" John asked, beginning to lose his patience.

"Like this!" Carson said, and he pulled Luz into a deep kiss.

No one on the set said a thing or moved a muscle. Luz' eyes were wide as she looked at Carson after the kiss. She didn't appear upset, just surprised. Carson looked surprised at himself.

He was looking at Luz and still holding onto her arms, then gently let go and turned away from her. He put his hand over his eyes, his head slightly bowed, then spoke. "It's a wrap. We'll use the first take. Take five," he said, and walked off the set, his face the color of a ripe pomegranate.

People still didn't move. They had just had a break right before the scene. Finally, some people began to whisper to each other.

John looked at Jillian, then walked over to her.

"I think you may be right about Carson," he said quietly as he reached her. He didn't want to say what she was right about as someone else might overhear it. Jillian just nodded.

"I'm sorry you had to watch all that—again," John added seriously, putting his hand on her shoulder.

"You were just doing what you were asked by your director. Anyway, I think I'm safe," she said with a smile.

She could tell John wanted to kiss her. "You are—but only because we're at work," he answered, smiling back and squeezing her shoulder.

"That's not exactly what I meant," she said, chuckling, then turning more serious. "What I was going to say is that I don't think Carson is on a one-way street."

"Really?" John asked.

"Really," Jillian answered and nodded. "And when I get a feeling like that..."

"I know—you are usually right," he said, still a bit unbelieving.

Carson picked up his bullhorn and directed the actors and crew to the next scene and set, where they filmed until five o'clock.

Two hours later, Greta sat across from Jillian in the breakfast nook, a blank look on her face. She wouldn't even have a cup of coffee—she said she had no desire for it anymore. Jillian had at least convinced her to have a glass of water.

"Greta," Jillian finally said. "I know that miscarrying is difficult for everyone, but I feel there is something else going on here. I don't know why I feel that way, but I do. Please, what can I do to help you?"

"No one can help me, Jillian." She sat quietly a moment, then she began to cry softly. "This is all my fault," she said.

Jillian waited a minute, but Greta said no more.

"What's makes you say that, Greta?" Jillian inquired gently.

"I didn't want to be pregnant!" she blurted out, and the tears really began to flow. Jillian let her cry. "We wanted to have a child—someday, just not right away. The baby was a surprise, and I wasn't ready for it."

Jillian knew how that felt.

"Drew was so excited—but I wasn't! All I could think of was myself—my new job opportunities, what they would say when they found out their brand-new professor was pregnant just as she was beginning a position with them. I didn't want this baby, and now he or she is dead—because of me!"

Jillian paused. "Greta, if that is how it works, there would be many more miscarriages in the world. There are many surprised new moms and dads out there, and they aren't always thrilled when they first get the word that they are going to be parents. It's scary enough when you are planning to be pregnant, but when you aren't, it is exceptionally daunting. You're looking at a person who wasn't expecting to be, or ready to be, a parent.

"And there are many, many people who wish they could get pregnant or stay pregnant, who want a baby so badly, and yet, it doesn't happen for them. We don't have all the answers to the whys and wherefores, but I don't believe you caused your miscarriage just because of your misgivings."

Jillian suddenly thought of Emma, the woman she had interviewed who was heading up a support group for people who miscarried or lost babies. The woman's husband had gone to pieces when she miscarried. He hadn't wanted a child yet, and thought it was his fault. Then they miscarried again, and he was even more convinced it was punishment for his earlier feelings. Finally, they had their little girl. Emma had begun the support group to help all parents grieving a loss and dealing with other feelings, like her husband's. It had taken him a long time to get over his grief and guilt. They had both gone to a support group on the other side of the city. After their experience, they decided to start one in their own area.

"Greta, I know someone I think you should talk to," she said. "Would you be willing to do that? I'll go with you if it would help, but I really think you, and then you and Drew, should speak with her." Jillian paused. "Does Drew know how you felt about being pregnant?"

"No. I just couldn't tell him. He was so excited. I wanted to be excited, too, but I just couldn't be—not yet. I feel like such a terrible person," she said.

Jillian put her hand on her arm. "Greta, you are a wonderful person. And you will be a wonderful mom—someday soon, when you are ready. But I really think your first step is to tell Drew how you felt, and how you feel now. Then, go see Emma, and hopefully get involved with her group, *Parents of Angels*."

"He's going to hate me," Greta said.

"Greta, there is no way on God's green earth that Drew could hate you," Jillian replied sincerely.

"Then he will be very disappointed in me," she said.

"I don't think that he will be that either. He might be disappointed about not being a dad as soon as he thought he would, but never with you. I've never seen him care about anything, or anybody, like he cares about you, Greta. You need to give him some credit."

Greta was quiet a moment. "You're right. I will tell him when I get home. I don't want to, but I...have to," she said.

"Yes, you do, for your sake, for his sake, and for your future's sake."

"How do I contact your friend?"

Jillian got the woman's card from her writing file and gave it to her, and told Greta to ask the woman about her own story. Greta nodded her head that she would.

They spent the next fifteen minutes talking about her physical health, with Jillian giving her a few pointers that worked for others she had known, and told her what made her feel better after she had had Marty.

Greta was even smiling weakly before she left, and Jillian got her to drink a glass of chocolate almond milk. She thought it would give her energy for her discussion with Drew that she promised to have the moment she got home.

They stood together by the front door of the house, when Greta suddenly hugged Jillian. "I felt like an awful human being when I came here tonight," she said, her eyes misting.

"Greta, you couldn't be an awful human being if you tried. I know that when you tell Drew, he will understand. And the more you share your feelings, the better you will feel, and the more able you will be to move forward. One of these days, you and Drew will *both* be ready to be parents. You will know when that time comes, and you will be a wonderful mom," Jillian said.

"Do you think so?" Greta asked.

"I know so," Jillian said, giving her a hug of affirmation.

Greta left, and Jillian said a prayer for this sweet, young woman, and for the talk she would have when she arrived home.

John bounded into the house at nine o'clock, not long after Greta had left.

"You seem chipper for someone who left the house nineteen hours ago," Jillian remarked as he walked toward her.

"We don't have to go in until noon tomorrow," John announced with a smile.

"How did that happen?" she asked, wrapping her arms around his neck.

"Carson said he had a meeting come up that he just couldn't miss," he said.

"I hope there aren't any problems with the production. We're pretty deep into all of this. They wouldn't pull the plug on us now, would they?" Jillian asked.

"I don't think that would happen. I just hope we don't have any big delays at the end of the production. I received a call this evening to audition for another play. Rehearsals would begin shortly after we are scheduled to be done with the movie."

"That's exciting," she said, gently tugging on his curls. For this movie, John had to grow his hair out again, even longer than he usually wore it. She loved how it turned up at his collar, and often found herself running her fingers through the wavy ends. "And speaking of exciting—how about the excitement on the set this morning?"

"That was something else, wasn't it?" John pulled her closer to him.

"I really do believe that Carson is falling in love with Luz. And from what I could tell, Luz didn't look like she minded his kiss too much," Jillian said.

John pulled her even closer. "Speaking of not minding a kiss..." he said softly.

Jillian smiled as she leaned into his embrace.

Carson's head was in a dense fog as he headed to his car. It was late, and there was only one other vehicle left in the lot, some sort of SUV parked next to his Tesla.

The day had been an absolute disaster in his book. The movie was going well, but his "display" in the morning with Luz was not only unprofessional but completely inexcusable. He had never lost control like that in this entire life. He had never been so embarrassed—at least not since he left North Dakota.

He hadn't been able to look Luz in the eye the rest of the day, and wondered if he would ever be able to again. He had called off the next morning's shoot, feigning an important meeting, just to try to gather his wits about himself. He had never done anything like that before either. *What is wrong with you?* He hung his head and looked at the concrete surface, walking slowly and dejectedly under the lot lights.

As he approached his car, he thought he saw something move. He stopped dead in his tracks. *Great, now you're probably going to get attacked to top off the day!* But no one came forward.

"Is someone there?" he asked in a cautious tone, still standing in the same spot, his eyes searching the dark shadows.

Slowly a figure moved out from the side of the SUV. He thought maybe he was dreaming as the person came into focus. It was Luz.

She walked up to him slowly. "I'm sorry if I frightened you," she said quietly. "I just wanted to see you—after what happened today."

Carson didn't know what else to say, so he just said, "I am so sorry, Luz..."

She interrupted him, stepping closer to him. "I didn't wait here all this time for an *apology,*" she told him.

Now Carson was really confused. "What did you wait here for, then?" he asked.

He inwardly panicked that she was about to quit her role in the movie. But instead, she put her hands on his upper arms. His heart began to pound against his chest. He could smell the sweet scent of her hair, and her dark eyes were flashing, just inches from his.

"This," she said. Then she gave him a kiss that made his earlier in the day look rather benign.

Drew was sitting in a chair in the living room, anxiously waiting for Greta to return home. She had texted him about her plans to meet with Jillian, and hadn't known how long she would be gone.

It was after nine, and he was just beginning to worry that something had happened to her when he heard the garage door open. He tried not to appear too eager as he approached the door to the attached garage, but he just couldn't seem to control himself and walked quickly toward the entrance.

Greta entered the room, saw him, and walked straight into his arms. He held her tightly.

They gently parted, and Greta looked into his eyes. "I have something I need to tell you," she said quietly, her eyes glistening.

"I'm all ears," he replied gently.

Over the next hour-and-a-half, Greta and Drew talked and cried, and talked and cried some more. Greta told him everything, and even Drew said he had been very surprised and unsure when he first found out about the baby. By the end of the night, they both had a plan to meet with the woman Jillian had recommended, and together they would attend the support group she facilitated.

"I feel like an elephant has been lifted from my chest," Greta said at the end of the evening. "Just being able to talk about it with someone...it made all the difference in the world. Jillian is sure a nice person. I can see why you dated her. But I don't understand why you chose me over her."

Drew put his arms around her. "Greta, I've never loved anyone—or anything—in my entire life like I love you," he said. "I am a different man because of you—just ask Jillian! You're the one for me, Greta, and no one else."

Chapter Eleven

Tommy rolled over and gazed at a sleeping Maria. He had hardly seen her in the past month, as there had been evening meeting after evening meeting. He spent more time with Amanda Richards than with his own family these days. That fact struck him hard, and he made a mental decision—the current situation needed to change. Amanda had continued her flattering remarks, and he continued to let her deliver them. He realized that this, too, needed to come to a halt—now.

There was yet another meeting scheduled for that evening. He put his hands behind his head, thinking about how to best manage the mess he'd gotten himself into. Maria stirred next to him, and her hand softly touched his chest. He reached down to hold it when he heard a knock on the door. It opened slowly, and Alison stuck her head into the room.

"Mom and Dad, remember I have to do my night driving practice tonight," she said with a big smile on her face. Then she disappeared down the hallway toward the bathroom. Alison was so excited about her driving sessions. Maria had been doing most of them with her lately. Even John Anthony had done one last week when both Tommy and Maria were busy with work. It was almost Alison's sixteenth birthday. She needed to get her driving hours in so she could pass her "behind-the-wheel" course, the last step before her road test.

Tommy sighed. He felt guilty for not being home again. "Can you do it?" he asked, looking at Maria, who had completely awakened once Alison began speaking.

"Another meeting?" she asked.

"Yes, I'm afraid so," he said, sighing again.

"You work so hard," Maria said, laying her head on his chest.

She was being so nice, it made him feel even more guilty. These meetings should have been over by now. It seemed to him that they were being stretched out longer than necessary, and he had gone right along with it. He would put an end to it. He prayed he would have the courage this evening.

Late that afternoon, Maria stopped by Tommy's office with two small coolers packed with food—one hot and one cold. Tommy's favorite was the "special of the day," and she brought two helpings, one for him and one for his business associate. The other cooler had two salads, two desserts, and two bottles of water. In a bag on the side was a small baguette of Italian bread.

Tommy was in a meeting with the CEO of the company when Maria arrived. She was just setting the coolers in Tommy's office when Amanda appeared at the door, looking for Tommy.

"Oh, I'm sorry," Amanda said. "I thought Tommy was here."

Maria's head jerked, hearing her husband called "Tommy" at work. No one in the office usually called him that. It was usually Mr. Romano, Thomas, or maybe Tom—never "Tommy."

"He's in a meeting with Mr. Francis," Maria said. "I was just leaving him and his associate some dinner."

"Oh, that's wonderful of you. I should introduce myself—Amanda Richards," she said, extending her faultlessly beautiful hand.

Maria felt stunned, as if she had been slapped, but extended her hand, feeling very self-conscious as she did so. All the cooking and cleaning up afterward had taken their toll on them since opening her business.

"Yes, my husband has spoken of you," Maria told her. *Except he left out the part about you looking like a cover girl.*

"And he, you," Amanda replied, her cornflower blue eyes and golden hair sparkling in the office lights.

"I should be going," Maria said. "Have a good meeting."

"Yes, all these night meetings. I wouldn't be able to tolerate them if it weren't for Tommy," Amanda said.

Maria wasn't sure what was worse, hearing his name spoken out of that perfect mouth, or the thought of Tommy with this gorgeous creature night after night.

"Good afternoon," Maria said, feigning a smile.

"Yes, it was wonderful to meet you," Amanda replied.

Maria thought about responding back the same, but just couldn't do it. She just kept going straight ahead toward the elevators. She had wished that she had dressed up more before she came to Tommy's office. She felt frumpy and old, although most people would feel that way when compared to the model-like beauty of Amanda Richards. The elevator doors opened, and she went inside. The doors closed, and she let out a heavy and worried sigh.

Maria stood at the kitchen counter cutting vegetables for dinner, but her mind was elsewhere.

"Ouch!" she exclaimed, as the sharp knife nicked her finger. She washed it quickly and wrapped it in paper towels. Maria hated sharp little cuts. It would very likely hurt for days and be a menace as she prepared meals at the shop.

While she was holding her finger upright and applying pressure, her cell phone went off. She glanced at the screen, saw that it was Jillian, and answered it. Anyone else outside of family would have had to wait.

Jillian asked her the usual "how are you?" She was just going to give the usual back—"fine," but needed to talk about the afternoon's events. She told Jillian the scenario at the office that afternoon.

"I think I can relate, Maria. I wasn't too happy when I found out my husband would be doing romantic scenes with Luz," she said honestly.

"Well, at least Tommy doesn't have to do anything like that..." she said, then stopped. She sure hoped he wasn't doing anything like that. She realized at that moment that she had never even given something like that a thought in all of their years together, and it made her feel terrible.

"Maria, are you okay?" Jillian asked after the pause.

"I think so," she said.

"You aren't worried about Tommy, are you?"

"No...I don't know. I never have been. But...you should see this woman. And we have been so busy lately at both of our workplaces..."

"Don't do that to yourself, Maria," Jillian said. "Tommy is a good man, and I know how much he loves you,"

"Yes, but he *is* human," Maria answered.

Alison walked into the room, and that was the end of that part of the conversation. Maria handed the phone to Alison and got a bandage for her finger.

Alison spoke with Jillian for a bit about some of her college choices and their planned road trip in just a month to visit them.

Alison wanted to go into nursing, like Jillian had, and had it narrowed down to a half of a dozen schools, including Jillian's alma mater, the University of Wisconsin.

When Maria returned to the room, Alison put the phone on speaker so they could both say goodbye. Jillian could hear the apprehension in Maria's voice, but there was nothing she could say with Alison right there. They said their goodbyes, then Jillian said a prayer for Maria and Tommy, two of her favorite people in the world.

Maria ate quietly as Alison chattered away about colleges. It was fun to see her so excited about the future, although Maria was in no hurry for her to leave home. It already seemed strange without John Anthony bounding into the house, dropping all his dirty, smelly workout clothes from whatever sport was currently in season, on the floor of the laundry room. She missed her son. She missed her family—their family.

The two of them cleared the table, put the food away and the dishes into the dishwasher. Then it was time for driving practice, as night was falling. Alison only needed one more hour of night driving to meet her requirements. Last week, they had gotten in the required "bad weather drive," courtesy of a spring rainstorm. It had been a bit nerve-racking, but they had returned home unscathed.

They began with Alison driving the streets in the neighborhood, then went across town, where it wasn't as familiar. Alison had to learn how to drive in places she hadn't been a million times. After forty-five minutes, they decided it was time to turn around and head back home. Maria was tired, and her mind just wasn't on the moment. She couldn't stop thinking about Tommy and his night meeting with Amanda Richards.

They came to a four-way stop sign. Alison looked both ways, and then proceeded to make a left-hand turn onto the street home. She wasn't sure where the car came from, but all of a sudden, there it was. It hadn't stopped at the stop sign. It didn't stop until it hit their car, just a bit behind the front passenger door. There was a sickening sound of metal crunching and glass breaking. Then it was silent.

Tommy and Amanda had enjoyed the meal that Maria had made—that is, until Amanda mentioned that she had met Maria when she dropped it off.

"You met Maria? When?" Tommy asked in a surprised voice.

"When you were in the meeting with Mr. Francis. I just happened to be stopping by to see…"

Tommy didn't hear the rest of what Amanda said. He was just wondering what his wife had thought when she met Amanda. He hadn't done anything wrong—or had he? He could have told her more about his new associate—given her a little bit of a "heads-up." And couldn't he and Amanda have hastened their pace at these meetings? And he could have told Amanda to stop with all the compliments, the tight-fitting clothes, the too-close-for-comfort distance she often had when talking or sitting next to him—a long time ago.

I shouldn't be here. I should be driving with Alison. He looked at the clock. Amanda walked toward him, her blouse unbuttoned a button or more than necessary, and leaned over the desk to get a paper, almost brushing against him.

"Amanda, don't do that," he said.

"Do what?" she asked, feigning innocence.

"We're done for tonight…in fact, we are done with this project *every night.* I have a family. I have a wife, and I need to go home…*now.*"

She looked at him in a surprised manner, then said coolly, "If that's the way you want it."

"Yes, it is. That is the way it is going to be, from this moment on," he replied, suddenly mustering the courage that had been missing the past few weeks.

"Good night then, Mr. Romano," she said, picking up her suit jacket and papers and heading to the door.

"Good night," he said.

Tommy looked at his watch. If he left now, he would probably make it home about the same time as Maria and Alison. They would have gone driving as soon as darkness fell, as it was a school night. He put the empty food containers away, put on his sport coat, and was about to grab the coolers when his cell phone rang.

Tommy tried to recall the officer's exact words when she called. He had blanked out for a moment. The last time he had gotten a similar call, his mother had been killed in a car accident. Now both his wife and daughter were at the hospital.

The officer, Sgt. Warren, had said that Alison had been lucky, and only sustained some minor bruises and cuts. They were, however, performing a concussion protocol with her just to be safe. His wife, they had said, had been on the side of the vehicle which had been struck by a car driven by an eighty-seven-year-old male who had very diminished night vision. He hadn't seen the stop sign until he was on top of it. He tried to brake, but it was too late. Luckily, he was not speeding, which helped. He was currently in intensive care, having suffered a heart attack after the accident. His car was an older model, well-built sedan, which had protected him well physically, but had totaled the Romano's car.

Maria had been knocked unconscious, had cuts and bruises— mostly from the airbags—and had symptoms of internal bleeding. Once she had come to, she had complained of abdominal pain. Her blood pressure was low, and her heart rate was rapid. The doctor would be making the decision about surgery shortly. By the time Tommy would get there, they would either still be doing tests, or if necessary, she would be on the operating table.

Tommy had called John and Jillian. They had offered to jump on a plane and come out, but Tommy told them to wait. The hardest call of all had been to John Anthony. He didn't need anything like this at the end of a school year. He had two more finals to go. If it hadn't been for Alison, he might not have called him—not yet anyway. But he thought that John Anthony might have to take his sister home.

Hot tears were gathering in Tommy's eyes. He couldn't believe he had put his entire family in this kind of jeopardy. His precious girl was hurt and must be completely traumatized. His son was being taken away from his studies in the middle of finals. He could hear the fear in John Anthony's voice on the phone. It had broken his heart. And his beautiful, sweet Maria...

The tears rolled down his cheeks, and his anger and guilt exploded in his mind. "Please God, don't let them pay for my mistakes," he prayed out loud.

John and Jillian finished a prayer for Maria, holding hands tightly as they sat on the love seat in the library. When they were done, Jillian spoke.

"I talked to Maria earlier this evening," Jillian said, suddenly thinking of the phone call. "I had just called to see how everything was going. She said that Tommy had another night meeting—one of many—with his new associate, a woman Maria had just met today, whom she described as looking like a model. She didn't sound very happy about the situation."

"She doesn't think that anything...inappropriate...is going on, does she?" John asked in a concerned tone.

"Not really, although she said they haven't seen each other much lately, and she did mention that Tommy is only human. I told her not to worry. I know Tommy loves her," Jillian said.

"Yes, he does. But I think I need to have a talk with my nephew—soon. I should be on a plane."

"It would be really tough for you to go, John, until filming is done Friday afternoon, but I do think someone should be with Tommy. I know how much different it felt when he arrived when you were in the hospital. Also, I would imagine that he feels terrible about being at work when this happened," Jillian said. "I'll go. I'm going to call Carson. He'll understand—and if not, I will make him understand."

John hugged her. "Thank you, sweetheart. I know Tommy will appreciate it, even if he said he doesn't need us. I'll call the travel agent and get you out of here ASAP, then book a flight for myself for the weekend. I think our family needs us," he said.

Jillian nodded, pulled out her cell phone, and hit "Carson Stone."

Carson was sitting in his car with the silent motor running. It was a good thing Jillian called, or he might have sat there until the battery died. Luz had kissed him—not just once, but twice. Then she said she would see him the next day at noon, and wondered if he had plans for dinner on Saturday evening.

He was pretty sure that he had said he had no plans, and agreed to meet Luz somewhere, but he just wasn't certain. He thought that perhaps it had all been a dream. He had watched her climb into the SUV that had been parked next to him and drive off. Then he had climbed into his car, where he was still planted.

"Carson," he answered in a dazed voice.

"Carson, it's Jillian," she said. Jillian relayed the family situation and asked if she could take off a few days, and said that she would be back to work on Monday.

"Fine—whatever you need to do, Jillian," he said in a strange tone.

Jillian really was beginning to wonder if the movie project truly was in jeopardy, for Carson to give her no fight in the matter whatsoever.

"Is everything all right, Carson?" she inquired, almost afraid to ask.

"I think so," he said.

"Okay. I will see you on Monday, barring any new developments."

"That would be wonderful," he replied, completely out of it.

Jillian didn't know what to say to his strange response, so she just said good night. She went upstairs to their room to get her small suitcase. She was packing when John came into the room.

"I take it everything went okay with Carson?" he asked.

"He said it was fine, but he also sounded like he was in another world," she said. "I hope there isn't some serious problem with the movie."

"If there is, we will deal with it. It's only a movie. There are more important things in life," he said, his eyes suddenly misty.

Jillian put her arms around him and hugged him tightly.

"It's going to be all right, John," she said. "I have a feeling that everything will turn out okay in the end." In her mind, she was thinking about more than just the injuries from the accident, but they would deal with one issue at a time. Right now, Tommy and John Anthony needed support, and Alison and Maria needed their prayers for good medical care and healing.

Chapter Twelve

Tommy sat on a chair pulled tight against Maria's bedside. He had finally convinced Alison to go home with John Anthony, who had arrived after speaking to his teachers. His son's professors had been wonderful, telling him to take all the time he needed to be with his family. At least Tommy didn't need to worry about that anymore.

After his children had gone home, Tommy had visited the chapel in the hospital. He remembered Jillian doing that when John was in the hospital. He thought that perhaps it was a good idea. He had been the only one there, which had been perfect, as he found himself on his knees. He proceeded to cry uncontrollably as he prayed for his wife—and prayed for forgiveness.

Now he looked at Maria's face. The doctor had performed an emergency splenectomy. Tommy gently put his hand on hers. He remembered the first time he ever touched her hand. It was on the way to the dance floor at the prom. It gave him shivers that night. It still gave him shivers. When they had danced, his heart had danced right along. By the end of the evening, which ended with their first kiss, he was a goner. He was completely and madly in love with the willowy girl with soft curls of light brown hair, and warm, light brown eyes to match.

He thought about how kind Maria had been that night at prom. She hadn't made fun of his awkward dance abilities, even though she must have had bruises on her feet by the end of the evening. But that was Maria. She never said a bad word about—or to—anyone. Everyone loved her—especially him.

He remembered the agonizing nights before they were married, when they would kiss and caress. Maria was a very devout girl, and had told him that she would not make love with him until it was their wedding day. Not even after their engagement would she change her mind, which was part of the reason they married while they were both still in school.

Thus, he had been shocked when at midnight twenty years before, there was a knock on his door. They had had their wedding rehearsal and dinner earlier, and afterward spent the evening with family at her parents' home. He had gone home to his apartment, which the next day would be their apartment. The knock had been so light that at first he thought someone was at his neighbor's, but then he heard it again. He went to the door wearing flannel pants and a T-shirt, wiping toothpaste from his lips with the bottom of the shirt.

Tommy had looked through the peephole, and there stood Maria. He hoped she was okay. He panicked for a moment, thinking that she had changed her mind and was going to call the whole marriage thing off. But when he opened the door, she looked at him in a way she had never looked at him before.

"It's our wedding day," she said softly. "I have to be back before dawn."

Tommy smiled at the memory, then tears returned to his eyes. His mother had once told him that "love like yours doesn't grow on trees, you know." He wondered what his mother would have said about all his evening meetings with Amanda Richards. He was pretty sure he knew, and he cried into his folded arms, his head touching Maria's side.

It was four a.m. when Jillian gently put her hand on Tommy's shoulder. He was still sitting on the chair pulled tight to Maria's hospital bed, bent over with his head next to her body on the mattress. The hand that had been holding Maria's now hung at his side.

His eyes opened, and he slowly sat up, groaning in pain from sleeping in such an awkward position. He turned his head and saw Jillian.

He pushed the chair back, stood up and hugged her, tears running down his face as he did. She just let him get it all out, as she was pretty sure it was what he needed to do. Finally, he stopped.

"It's all my fault," he said quietly.

"She looks like she is resting peacefully. Let's talk in the family room," Jillian responded softly.

They walked a few doors down to a small room with a couch and sat down.

"First of all, how is Maria?" Jillian asked.

"She has a concussion, bruises, and cuts—and they had to take out her spleen," he said, his voice beginning to break. "And it's all my fault."

"Tommy, it is not your fault. From what you told me, a gentleman who shouldn't have been driving at night was doing just that," she said.

"I know, but if I hadn't been at work..."

"If you hadn't been at work, it might have been you instead of Maria. That's possible. Or Alison wouldn't have been on the same street at the same time. But that doesn't mean it was your fault."

"I shouldn't have been gone. I've been gone too much lately. It should have been me, not her. I shouldn't have had another night meeting with..." He stopped, looking ashamed.

"With your new associate?" Jillian asked.

Tommy looked surprised. "How did you know?"

"I had called Maria last night around dinnertime. She mentioned that you were at a meeting—and that she had met your new co-worker earlier," she said.

"Was she upset?" he asked.

"I'm not sure I would use that word. She mentioned that the woman was very pretty. She also mentioned that you have had a lot of meetings lately," Jillian said honestly.

They were silent a moment.

"Jillian. I don't know what I would do if I lost Maria. I love her so much. And my associate—I've spent way too much time with her. I've let her flatter me way too much, too. But nothing else—not that those things aren't bad enough," he said.

"I believe you, Tommy," Jillian replied. "Now, you have to stop blaming yourself, and get to work on helping Maria heal—in every way."

He just nodded his head, his eyes teary.

"I'm so glad you're here, Jillian," he said finally.

"Me, too," she responded, hugging this man whom she loved like a brother.

Tommy and Jillian returned to Maria's room after their talk. Tommy resumed his post at Maria's side, and there was no way he was going to leave it. Jillian parked herself in a recliner in the corner of the room and drifted off to sleep, until she awakened to a voice around seven a.m.

"Hi, beautiful," she heard Tommy say to his wife.

Maria's eyes were open, and Tommy was hovering above her face. Jillian came to the bedside. She said hello, squeezed Maria's hand, and told them she was going to make a call to John, which was the truth. It was also a good excuse to give them some time alone, not unlike what Tommy had done with her and John when he was hospitalized.

Tommy had trouble speaking at first. He held Maria's hand tightly, then kissed it gently.

"Maria...," he said softly, struggling to find words, and searching her face. "I...I..."

"Shhh. Do me a favor?" she said in a weak voice.

"Anything. What do you need?" Tommy asked.

"A kiss," she said, surprising him.

He smiled through his tears. "That I can do," he said, moving toward her face. It reminded him of their first kiss—tentative at first, then sweet and building. If he could have, he would have climbed into the bed beside her.

She smiled at him again. "How is our girl?" she asked, still holding his hand tightly.

"She is just fine," said a voice from the doorway. There stood John Anthony and Alison with a bouquet of flowers in a familiar vase, picked from the late spring flower beds in the backyard of their home. Maria would often pick them and put them in this very same vase for special occasions.

Alison put the vase into John Anthony's hands and rushed to her mother's side.

"Mom, I'm so sorry," she said, beginning to cry as she hugged Maria.

"There's nothing to be sorry about, honey," Maria answered, stroking her daughter's hair. "It's called an accident. They happen all the time. I didn't see that other car either, and I've been driving for many years." She didn't want to mention that she might have seen it if her mind hadn't been in another place, although at the rate of speed the other car was going, there may not have been anything she could have possibly done.

"I'll probably never get my license now," she said.

Maria looked at Tommy.

"You were not given a citation, so that's a good sign. We will figure it out, Alison. Right now, we just have to get your mom on the mend," her father said encouragingly.

"Now that all my wonderful family is here, that should be no problem at all," Maria said, trying to reassure them.

John Anthony put the flowers down on a small table next to the hospital bed, and joined his mom, his dad, and his sister in a huge family hug.

Jillian watched from the door of the hospital room, tears of happiness in her eyes. She loved this family—now her family, too.

After an hour, Jillian suggested that she, John Anthony, and Alison go home. Maria needed her rest. She also knew that Tommy and Maria needed some time alone together and John Anthony needed to get back to his studies. Alison needed to rest and also do her makeup homework to get ready for school the next day, which thankfully, was Friday. That made Jillian smile, as she realized that meant that late the next night, John would arrive.

Jillian made some cinnamon-vanilla French toast for two grateful young people when they arrived back at the house. It reminded her of Marty's high school and early college years, with conversations revolving around exams, concerts, and summer plans. She had missed those days and had thought they were all in the past. Now she was basking in her role as "Aunt Jillian," getting to share special moments with her newly inherited family.

John Anthony reluctantly left after breakfast, but knew that he could come back that evening to visit his mom. He also knew that he wanted to finish his semester as soon as possible. Alison wondered if it would be all right if she went back to bed for a while before doing her homework. Jillian was actually thrilled with that idea, as that meant that she, too, could catch a nap. The brief one in the recliner at the hospital had been welcomed, but its benefits had now worn off. It would feel great to close her eyes and stretch out in a real bed for a bit.

At the hospital, Tommy would not leave Maria's side. At one point, Maria mentioned that it was okay if he wanted to go home and sleep, or even nap in the recliner in the room, but he wouldn't hear of it.

"I've spent too much time away from you lately. That will never happen again if I can help it," he said, squeezing her hand. She smiled at him, then drifted off into a peaceful sleep.

A taxi pulled up at Tommy and Maria's residence at midnight the following night. Out stepped a weary John. He brightened as he saw Jillian and Tommy waiting for him at the door to the house. He quickly paid the cabbie and practically jogged up the sidewalk.

"I'm not sure whom to hug first," he said with a huge grin and setting down his carry-on.

Jillian stepped back. "Since I get that privilege on a regular basis, go for it!" she said, nodding her head toward Tommy.

The two men embraced and kissed. Jillian's eyes felt hot and watery as she watched her favorite two men in the world share their affection. They were more like father and son than uncle and nephew.

"Okay, Zio. It's Jillian's turn," Tommy said with a big smile on his face, grabbing John's suitcase and taking it inside.

John held Jillian and looked into her eyes. They had only been apart about forty-eight hours, but it had seemed like a lifetime to both of them. He kissed her slowly, then pulled her close.

Kathy J. Jacobson

"Boy, I didn't get a kiss like that," Tommy said teasingly.

It made Jillian feel good that Tommy actually felt like joking, and that he had actually agreed to come home for the night. If John had not been arriving, it may have been more difficult to convince him. She could sense his relief and hopefulness as his support network continued to grow.

"I would hope not," Jillian said, teasing right back.

The three sat at the kitchen table and talked for a short time, but they were three exhausted people and knew the morning would be upon them quickly. John mentioned to Tommy that if everything was going well the next afternoon, he wouldn't mind taking a trip out to the cemetery in Belvidere. Jillian said she would stay with Maria if they did that.

The doctors had told Tommy that if Maria kept progressing in the current manner, with no complications, she might be able to go home Sunday at noon—Monday at the latest. Tommy had already contacted his office and told them he would not be in until further notice.

His supervisor hadn't been too happy about it, but Tommy reminded him that he was using his sick leave benefits for the first time in his eighteen years of work with the firm. His boss had no further comments after that reminder, and simply wished Maria well. Tommy was a bit surprised by his boss' attitude. It didn't used to be like that. It used to be like working with family, but in the last year or so, he felt they were losing that feeling. It seemed his company was becoming more about profits than people these days. The realization made him feel disappointed and sad.

When Tommy, John and Jillian arrived at the hospital the next morning, Maria was not in her room. At first Tommy panicked, but Maria appeared at the door a moment later, returning from a walk with a nursing assistant.

"Looking for someone?" asked the familiar voice.

Tommy whipped around. "Thank goodness!"

Maria and the assistant, who was holding onto her, slowly entered the room.

She stopped to give John a hug, a huge smile on her face. "What a girl has to do to get a visit from her favorite people from California!" she said.

"We will try to come more often so you don't have to go to such drastic measures next time, Maria," John replied, grinning from ear to ear.

The assistant helped Maria back into the bed slowly. Maria winced as she tried to get into a comfortable position, her tender abdominal area protesting. She let out a deep breath once she finally found a reasonable spot.

They had left Alison at home, as they wanted her to get some sleep. The four of them talked a bit about the accident. The man who hit Alison and Maria's car had survived his heart attack, although they had nearly lost him at one point. His wife had stopped by to see Maria just before her walk. She had apologized to her, mentioning that her husband rarely drove at night, but that night she had had a terrible cough. She had recently given up driving altogether, and her husband had insisted on getting her some cough syrup, so he ventured out to the store. It was only two miles from their home and he had promised to be extra careful. When she said that, the woman had broken down crying, and Maria cried right along with her.

Already two lawyers had contacted Maria about suing the poor man. She wanted nothing to do with something like that. Her insurance agent had already mentioned that her car would be completely covered and that there would be a significant amount given to her for additional pain and inconvenience. That seemed like adequate compensation to her.

She was a bit worried about work, however, but Tommy reassured her that the "troops" were rallying. All of her employees had gathered together the first morning with the new cook she had recently hired and had made a plan, at least through the next week. They were all going to put in extra hours and do their best to keep things up to par. Tommy said that they mentioned that she always treated them so well—paying good wages, giving them benefits, and caring about them as people. Now it was their turn to return the favor.

Still, she wondered how long they could go on without her. She sincerely hoped she would be back on her feet in time for "Out to Lunch." It would be her first year as a vendor at the summer food and music event held on Fridays in downtown Libertyville's Cook Park. She could feel the stress building in her mind.

This time away would also delay her search for a business manager. The other day she had decided that she had to give some things up. She needed to spend more time with her family. She was happy that her business was doing so well, but not happy about the time she was gone from home. Even when she was home, she was completely worn out. She needed someone to do the bookwork and take care of the other business aspects of the shop, so she could concentrate on cooking and the people she served in the community, and most importantly, the people she loved at home.

Tommy, John, and Jillian returned to the house at noon. Tommy whipped up some sandwiches, and then they made a plan.

John and Tommy would drive to Belvidere after dropping Jillian and Alison off at the hospital. They would return before dinnertime, then play dinner "by ear." It all depended on how Maria was feeling, and how much company she could handle.

Jillian had reminded them all that a lot of company wasn't always a good thing, even if people meant well.

John and Tommy headed due west on I-90. They had a little over an hour drive ahead of them—a perfect amount of time for a good talk. John drove the car so Tommy could talk without having to concentrate on driving. He thought his nephew might have a few things weighing on his heart, and he was right.

"I almost lost the best thing in my life, Zio. And I'm not talking about the accident," he admitted. "How do you do it...with all those beautiful women you have to work with—and even do love scenes...?"

"I'll admit, in my younger years it was...interesting, let's say. But I didn't have someone special in my life then...someone I couldn't live without...like I do now," John said. "I never thought I could love anyone the way that I love my wife."

Tommy nodded his head. "I understand that feeling. That's why I am so upset with myself."

"Tommy, you made a mistake. But you're going to have to get over it. Life is too short. We have to put to rest our resentments and our disappointments. We need to forgive—even forgive ourselves," John said.

Tommy was silent after that, and John could tell he was mulling things over.

They arrived at the cemetery. John grabbed a little bag he had brought with him, along with a trowel, some paper towels, a small ruler, and rubbing alcohol he had borrowed from Tommy before they left the house.

"This won't take long," John said, as they walked on the lush green grass to the graves of John's grandparents, parents, and brother Anthony and his wife, Tommy's parents.

They stood in front the graves, which were all in a row in a shady area of the cemetery. John stopped at the foot of his parents' grave and stood silently. After a moment, he carefully reached into his bag and pulled out a small package, wrapped in bubble wrap. In it was a photo on a ceramic disc. It was a copy of the photograph his second cousin, Pietro, had given him in Italy on his wedding trip.

He unrolled a few paper towels, and carefully prepared a spot in the center of the gravestone, near its top.

"Do you think this would look good right here, Tommy?" John asked, holding the tile up to the area he had just wiped clean.

Tommy just nodded, too emotional to speak. John measured the space to make sure it was accurately centered, then asked Tommy to stand back and make certain he had it just right before he pressed it on. The industrial-grade adhesive on the back would not be removable once in place.

When they were sure it was in the correct position, John pressed it on firmly. Then they both stood back, their eyes fixed on the photo of John and Anthony's parents, holding their young sons, and smiling adoringly at one another.

John nodded his head affirmatively at the photo, with watery eyes. "Now, for my big brother," he said, opening up his sack once more. He pulled out a small wooden box, opened it gently, and turned to Tommy. "I hope you don't mind, but I'd like to give this to your father," he said, his voice beginning to break.

In a box lined with red velvet, lay the figure of the baby Jesus— the one from the beloved family crèche. John and Anthony had fought over which one of them got to put the baby Jesus in the manger every Christmas Day—even coming to physical blows at times, usually behind their parents' backs. Their parents finally made them draw straws, but the loser always had given the winner some sort of payback, even if the honor had been given "fair and square."

John took the trowel and began digging a small hole near the top of the gravesite, on the side where his brother's remains rested. He closed the small box and gently laid it in, covering it with the soft, warm earth. "There you go, Anthony," he said, patting the top of the small patch of dirt with his palm one more time.

John stood up and took a few steps back. He stopped at the foot of the two graves, his head bowed, with tears gently rolling down his cheeks. Tommy stood beside him, joining his uncle with his own lowered head, prayers, and waterworks.

Finally, John crossed himself, and Tommy followed suit. John picked up the empty bag at his feet, put the dirty trowel in it, and picked up the roll of paper towels, ruler, and rubbing alcohol. He wiped away his tears and then smiled at his nephew. Tommy nodded and smiled back. They walked back to the car together, John extending his arm around Tommy's shoulders.

For the first part of the return ride, both of them were quiet. Later, Tommy began to talk about work. He had been bothered by his supervisor's attitude about his current family situation. There had been a time when his workplace had felt like another family, but not anymore.

John spoke about what a blessing it was to be "self-employed." If a work situation was really bad, he just wouldn't associate with a particular production company or director in the future. He also told Tommy how wonderful it was to work with Jillian. He was very proud of her writing, her medical expertise, and what he thought was a natural talent for direction. He had noticed that Carson used her suggestions more and more often, acknowledging that they were creative ideas or improvements.

"Do you ever feel like it's too much—being together all day and every night, and bringing the office home with you, as they say?" Tommy asked.

"Honestly, Tommy, I don't think I could ever get too much of Jillian. Maybe there will come a day, but I highly doubt it. And as for 'the office,' we both seem to be able to know when enough is enough, and can turn our discussions when needed."

Tommy was quiet the rest of the way home, thinking again. He was a lot like his uncle in that department. He liked to think things through—process them.

John and Tommy found Maria, Alison, and Jillian laughing when they entered the hospital room. Maria was holding a pillow to her stomach as she giggled.

"Tommy, help! You have to get these two out of here before I rupture my sutures and staples!" Maria cried.

Tommy smiled and leaned over to kiss her. He and John were beaming.

"You two must have had a good afternoon," Maria said.

"Why do you say that?" Tommy asked.

"It's written all over your faces," she replied, and Jillian and Alison nodded in agreement.

"We did," Tommy acknowledged. "I'll tell you all about it when you get home. Any word from the doctor?"

"You just missed him. It looks like I will able to leave right before lunch tomorrow," she said, glowing.

"That's wonderful," Tommy replied, picking up her hand, then kissing it.

"That is, if I get enough rest," Maria said. "Really, I think you all should go to dinner. John Anthony should be free soon. He called to say he was going to take his second exam this afternoon. He didn't think he could be any more ready than he is right now, so he called his professor and set it up. I would imagine he would be up for a celebration after two exams in one day, including the final one of the semester!"

"Are you sure, hon?" Tommy asked.

"I am—really. Just promise me you will come and get me

tomorrow! And don't forget to go to church. And please thank Father Pat. He came while you were all home for lunch, and prayed for me and gave me communion," she said.

"We will," everyone said in unison, which made Maria clutch her pillow once more.

"Oh, you people! Out with you!" she said, chuckling.

They each took turns giving her a hug and a kiss goodbye, Tommy bringing up the rear.

"I love you, Maria, so much," he said after kissing her.

"I love you, too, Tommy," she said, her eyes and voice full of affection.

The family ate at a popular brewpub on Milwaukee Avenue in Libertyville. They dug into their thick burgers and fries, and laughed when Alison commented that they were all eating like a pack of ravenous wolves.

"It's a sign of relief," Jillian said. They all nodded in unison. Between the accident, Maria's emergency surgery, finals, and last-minute trips across the country, it had been an unusually crazy week for everyone.

They stopped for a tub of their favorite ice cream on the way home, then sat around the kitchen table finishing it off and talking until almost midnight. They could have talked longer, but they were all tired and they were going to the earlier church service so they would not be late in bringing Maria home.

Jillian, John, and Alison planned to go back to the house after worship, to straighten up and make some lunch while Tommy and John Anthony picked up Maria. Maria couldn't wait to have "real food" again, as she put it, so they wanted to have everything ready for her when she returned.

John and Jillian practically fell into the comfy guest room bed, sinking into the ultra plush mattress. John turned to Jillian, putting his hand on her arm.

"I'm so glad we came," he said.

"So am I," she agreed, moving her hand to stroke his rough cheek. She loved that feeling. "So—today?" Jillian asked, curious about the excursion to Belvidere.

John told Jillian what he had done. He had mentioned a month or so earlier that the next time they went to Illinois, he wanted to go to the cemetery where his family was buried. She hadn't known exactly why, but now her eyes were brimming as he told his story of reconciliation.

"You're not upset about baby Jesus, are you?" John asked.

Jillian's hand slid to the back of his head. "I think that's one of the nicest things you've ever done, Mr. Romano. Both of them. Only a special person could think of doing things like that. I'm so proud of you, John," she said softly, fingering his curls, and moving her face closer to his.

He smiled. Jillian knew how much John wanted her to be proud that she married him. He had nothing to worry about in that department, not in her eyes anyway. She would cherish this man for the rest of their lives together.

"I'm glad," he said. They said their nightly refrain to each other, then John pulled her into a kiss.

Maria cried when she crossed the threshold of her house, holding onto Tommy's strong arm. "I'm home," she said, smiling through her tears. "I wasn't sure..." She didn't finish her sentence. She didn't want to upset Alison, who was only a step behind her, carrying in the empty vase from the flowers she and John Anthony had brought to the hospital. *Home. Thank you God, I am home.*

Jillian and John had made a healthy and fabulous lunch of a grilled chicken and avocado salad, served in soft, fresh pita bread, with melon slices on the side. Everyone sat at the table together, Maria in a chair with sides, with one pillow beneath her and another at her back. She remarked that she felt like a queen, as everyone hovered around her, jumping up to get whatever she felt like eating or drinking. She claimed she could get used to this type of treatment quite easily.

After lunch, Maria gingerly pushed herself up from her chair and walked to the couch, where she eventually settled into a comfortable position to rest. John, Jillian, Tommy, Alison, and John Anthony cleared the table, washed the dishes, countertops, and dining table. Then it was time for John and Jillian to pack their bags and go to the airport.

It was never easy to say goodbye to their family, but this time was exceptionally tough. They took turns with each member of the family, with hugs, kisses, and words of encouragement abounding. They ended with a very emotional and appreciative Tommy and Maria. The blare of a taxi's horn sounded loudly through a screen on the open living room window, and reluctantly John and Jillian were off and back to their world.

Chapter Thirteen

It had only been a short time since John and Jillian left Los Angeles, but it felt like a lifetime. And when they returned to the set Monday morning, they thought perhaps they truly had been gone a lifetime, or perhaps had landed on a different planet. Something had definitely happened over the past few days, as Carson Stone was like an alien to them—in a good way.

He had shed the boots he had been wearing for the past few weeks and was back to his signature loafers. But there was more than that—much more. Jillian couldn't quite put her finger on it until she got up close to him. It was his eyes. They seemed so different that she wondered if they had miraculously changed color. But they were the same cool blue, only they twinkled. They looked like they were smiling. He talked with her for a moment and even his voice sounded like it was smiling! Jillian thought to herself that there could only be one explanation—Luz.

When Jillian went over to speak with Luz a short time later, Jillian's conviction was even stronger. There was the same sparkle in Luz' dark eyes that she had seen in Carson's. It was pure and simple. The two had the eyes of love.

Jillian was brought back into the moment by the sound of Carson's voice.

"Directors' meeting at the end of filming today!" he announced.

Jillian felt bad that John would have to wait for her, but he said not to worry, he would relax in the lounge. She hoped the meeting wouldn't be too long, because she also wanted to speak to Carson privately after the meeting.

The filming went smoothly all day. There were no more demonstrations about how to kiss, no more put-downs, no more static of any type on the set by Carson—or anyone, for that matter. They were heading into the final weeks of the project, with two on-location shoots coming up, but neither very far away. The final one would be at Yosemite National Park. Jillian was looking forward to that one, as she hadn't been there yet. The filming would end just in time for their "day in court"—adoption day for both Rick and Marty.

Jillian smiled as she thought about the big event, which would happen shortly before Marty and Michael took their boards, and then after which they would leave for Lima.

"You look happy," a familiar voice said in her ear that afternoon.

Without even turning, she answered her husband, "That would be an understatement."

Jillian felt very blessed that day. It had been wonderful to see Tommy and his family, even under scary circumstances. She felt confident when they left that Maria would be okay, and even more so, that Maria and Tommy would be "okay." Jillian's heart had swelled, too, at John's gestures of love and forgiveness toward his father and brother. And now, the movie was beginning to wrap up, and soon her daughter would have a real father—a legal one, who loved her and wanted her—for the first time in her life. There was *a lot* to smile about.

❖

At the end of the day, John slipped Jillian the car keys and told her he had found a ride home with another actor, if she didn't mind. Jillian didn't mind a bit. She knew that John was exhausted, because she was exhausted, too. But duty called. She wearily made her way to Carson's office, a fresh cup of coffee in her hand.

Carson wanted to talk about the on-location filming and suggestions for making everything go as smoothly as possible. Jillian reminded him to have a good first-aid kit along this time, in case there was another incident like the one in Alaska, when Chase Cheekwood dislocated his finger.

Carson groaned and said he sincerely hoped they wouldn't experience anything remotely like that scenario again, but typed "first-aid kit" into his tablet. At least this time there was civilization close by, just in case there was some sort of emergency.

The meeting lasted an hour-and-a-half, then everyone began to leave. Jillian purposely lagged behind. She wasn't sure how to bring up the subject, so she simply asked Carson a question.

"Would you and Luz like to join us for dinner some night soon?" she asked, a sly smile spreading across her face.

Carson's head jerked back a bit. He was trying to not look surprised, but quickly gave up.

"How did you know?" he asked quietly.

"It's pretty obvious that you two 'have it bad,' as my mother used to say," she said.

"Why do you say that?" he asked, trying to play it cool, but also sounding hopeful.

"Last week you were jumping down her throat, and she could barely look at you. Now you can barely keep your eyes off one another, and both of you have the 'look of love,' for lack of a better phrase."

Carson shook his head. "I never thought something like this... someone like her...it's a miracle, Jillian," he said so seriously.

"I don't think it's that miraculous when one nice, talented, and intelligent person falls in love with another nice, talented, and intelligent person," she said.

"But Luz..."

"Luz is human, just like the rest of us," Jillian said.

"You are right, Jillian. She did tell me the other night how many people forget that. They don't realize how she's been treated—or I should say, mistreated—by people, especially men."

"I can believe that. I would imagine she has had some really negative experiences that the rest of us who are not in the 'most beautiful people in the world' category could ever imagine," Jillian said.

"Yes, she alluded to some of those. I'd like to knock their heads off," Carson said, "and I've never thought, or said, words like that before in my life, Jillian."

"I understand, Carson. So, again, please talk to Luz and let me know when you two would like to come over for dinner," Jillian said, picking up her empty coffee cup and her tablet. "Carson, I'm so happy for you—for both of you," she added with a smile.

He smiled back. "Good night, Jillian. And thank you."

When the door closed, Carson twirled around in his chair and looked out the glass walls at the Hollywood hills, his mind drifting back two nights before.

The day after Luz had kissed him in the parking lot, she had cornered him at the end of the day and slipped him a piece of paper. All day they had tried to keep their eyes off of one another, quite unsuccessfully. Written on the paper were instructions about where and when to meet her the following night. He was to meet her at a Peruvian restaurant at seven o'clock. He should park in an alley in the back. There would be someone there who would then escort him into the restaurant through the back door. She would meet him inside.

On Saturday, he had changed his clothes a ridiculous number of times. How did one dress to go to dinner with someone like Luz? He finally decided he needed to go to a store. He hadn't bought any clothes in a very long time, and he was sure that everything he had was outdated, unless it was old enough to have come back in style.

The gentleman at the first shop he had gone into was very rude. He quickly made an exit, then called an acquaintance who always looked well-dressed and asked him where he usually did his shopping. His friend sounded shocked that Carson wanted to buy something new, but gave him the name of the shop and whom to ask for, and told Carson to give the sales associate his name.

That did the trick. The salesperson was very professional and patient. He could sense that this was something new for Carson, or "Mr. Stone," as he called him. Carson ended up buying a suit, a sport jacket and slacks, three shirts, three ties, and a new pair of dress shoes. The salesman gave him suggestions for what to wear on an important date. Carson was very grateful for the consultation, especially later when he saw Luz' approving gaze as he walked toward their table.

At first, he was a bit confused. There was no one else in the restaurant. He looked around as he walked through the empty room. She was sitting at a small round table. There were burning candles on the table, and on all of the tables, but no other diners.

He was going to say something about it being a quiet night, but when Luz stood up to greet him, he could barely think straight, let alone speak. She was wearing a very simple black dress, in a modest cut compared to her usual attire. Other than the night at the Romanos, he had never seen her in anything other than brightly colored, overly figure-accentuating dresses before. He thought she was stunning, her dress matching her hair and eyes, which were glowing in the candlelight.

He gently reached out his hand to hers. She reached out hers to meet his, and he lifted it to his lips and gently kissed it, his eyes never leaving hers.

"Hi," he said quietly. He was usually more formal, but considering the way he felt, he was lucky to get a word out.

"Hola," she said, and smiled at him. "Should we sit?"

"Yes, of course," he replied, and pulled her chair out for her to sit down. She looked pleasantly surprised.

"I wanted you to get a taste of my country's cuisine this evening. I also wanted to be able to talk to you, and you know how difficult that would be under normal circumstances, so I rented the restaurant for my own private party tonight—a party of two," she said, smiling in a way that made him feel weak in the knees.

Carson felt surprised, and then honored. "How thoughtful," he said.

A young woman and gentleman came out to speak with them. The man would be their server. The woman was their chef. They discussed the options for dinner, and Chef Ramona asked if Carson had any dislikes or food allergies. She was pleased when he informed her that he had no allergies and was open to any and all suggestions that evening. Luz told them a few items she really wanted Carson to try, then mentioned that any others were up to the chef.

Over the next four hours they ate and talked, and ate and talked. Carson had never been so open about his life with anyone. He ended up telling her everything—including being left at the altar by his fiancée, Cindy, and how afterward he left his home state and had never looked back.

Luz talked about what it was like to grow up being the tallest girl in her class. Both boys and girls made fun of her. Even her own father made fun of her. He was a verbally abusive man, and sometimes physically abusive when he drank too much.

Later, when she developed early at age thirteen, other problems began. She was assaulted by an uncle, and had date after date disrespect her. The other girls in school were jealous of her beauty and spread rumors about her, which didn't help. She couldn't wait to get away.

When she was sixteen, she was "discovered" while working at a dress shop in Lima. An actress had come to shop one day. The woman's boyfriend, who was a movie producer, stopped in to take the actress and her many shopping bags home. The actress was still changing when he arrived, and he milled about the shop impatiently.

Luz was putting the clothing back that the actress did not want to buy, when the director noticed her and stopped dead in his tracks. He had a good eye for natural beauty and for people others might want to see on the screen, so he immediately invited Luz to come to the studio the next day. She was hired instantly and groomed to be the newest, hottest star in the country of Peru, then the rest of South America—and later, the world. All along the way, she explained, men repeatedly disrespected her and used her.

They each shared their personal stories, listening attentively to one another. At eleven o'clock, Luz mentioned they should leave and let the restaurant staff close for the night. Carson wanted to pay for the evening—or at least share the bill—but Luz would not hear of it.

"This has been the nicest evening," Luz said, as she stood up.

Carson stood up, went behind her, and pulled her chair back for her. Luz turned to move from the chair, then she turned toward Carson.

His heart was thundering again—being so close to her. But this time it wasn't just her outward beauty that made him feel that way

—it was all of her. She was such an amazing person. Why anyone would treat her so poorly...he could not fathom it.

They looked at one another, each waiting for the other to make the first move. Finally, at the very same time, they moved slowly toward one another, and their lips met. It was a long and gentle kiss, different than their previous ones.

When they parted, Luz quietly said, "Your Cindy—what a fool."

Carson put his forehead to hers for a moment and smiled.

"I will see you at work Monday morning," Luz said.

Carson wanted to kiss her again, but he also didn't want to ruin what had been the best night of his life, so he nodded, kissed her hand, said good night, and headed to the back door. He hadn't been able to stop smiling all the way home. He still couldn't stop smiling, period.

He said he would call Luz tonight and find out if she would like to go to John and Jillian's with him, but he didn't have to wait to call her, as she was waiting outside his door when he opened it to go home. That brought yet another huge smile to his face.

The ride home seemed particularly long and lackluster without John at Jillian's side. She had actually enjoyed commuting to and from the studio with him, even with their pre-dawn departures. Even rush-hour traffic didn't seem so bad when they were together. But tonight—this was really a *pain*. She was stuck in a long line of cars.

Jillian turned on the radio and adjusted the rearview mirror out of boredom. She looked into the mirror—and that's when she saw it. Her head snapped back as she noticed a familiar vehicle two cars behind in the lane next to her. It was an old silver Buick. Her heart began to pound. She turned off the radio and sat for a moment, just thinking about what to do. She decided at the next opportunity, she would turn off onto a different route home, using a back way—that was, if she ever got off this infernal freeway. If it really was the same car, and if it really was following her, it would have to go out of its way as well.

Half an hour later, she got off at the nearest exit. She heard honking behind her. The silver car was crossing over two lanes to exit as well. She wondered if she should try calling John, but what could he do? Then she thought she should call their security company and see what they suggested.

The security manager told her to go straight home. They would have a white unmarked van parked near the entrance to her property with officers inside. She should stop outside the gate, but not go in, unless the car went on. If it stopped, the officers would approach the driver.

She felt like she was in one of the studio's movie scenes, as she snaked through the streets on the way home. The Buick kept its distance, but it was definitely following her. Why would someone follow her? John, she could understand, but her?

Jillian finally made it to the gate of her home and pulled up, but did not hit the code to enter. She turned her head slightly to see if the car was coming. It was way at the end of the block, slowly moving her way. She continued to sit there as it kept approaching. Her heart sounded in her ears. She should have called John—just in case. What if something happened to her? She could have told him that she loved him...

The car pulled up slowly behind the white van and stopped. A man opened the door, climbed out, and stood up. Something looked vaguely familiar about him, but she didn't see him for more than a second before the two security officers, one with a gun in his hand, quickly approached him.

Now Jillian really felt like she was in a movie scene. The officer without a weapon pulled out a radio. The man from the Buick put his hands up, seeing a gun pointed right at him. Jillian just sat frozen, then watched as one of the officers came to her window.

"He's says he knows you. You're old friends or something—from back in Milwaukee," the security officer said in a doubting tone.

Milwaukee. Who would be here from Milwaukee?

The security officer said he had patted the man down, and he appeared to have no weapons, so she slowly opened her door. As she approached the scene, she could see the man trembling as the other guard was still pointing the weapon at him, now standing at an even closer range. She thought the guard was enjoying this entire thing a bit too much, and she asked him to holster his weapon. He reluctantly did so and moved back a few steps as she approached.

Who was this man? There was something familiar about him, but she just couldn't put her finger on it.

"Jillian?" the man asked so quietly she could barely hear him.

"Yes," she responded tentatively.

"Jillian Johnson? Who used to be a parish nurse in Milwaukee?" he asked in a stronger voice.

Hearing that stronger, more confident voice, she suddenly knew exactly who he was. Gone was the thick, wavy auburn hair. Instead, just a few light wisps of gray hair stretched across his otherwise bald scalp. He was at least fifty pounds heavier than the last time she had seen him. His eyes, which had once been among the brightest, piercing blue eyes she had ever encountered, looked old and dull.

"Scott?" she asked, her head reeling a tad.

"Yes, it's me," he said, looking down at the ground.

Scott Bradford. The second man who had shattered Jillian's heart. She had once loved this man. She had once thought that she would marry this man. He had been the new pastor in the parish, the widower every woman in church was gaga over. It turned out he felt the same way about many of them, and he had been dismissed for clergy misconduct, leaving a shattered congregation, along with Jillian's matching heart.

She looked at the officers, and they backed off to give them some breathing room. The officer with the gun spoke. "We'll be right here, ma'am, if you need us. We'll be watching," he added, looking straight at Scott.

After the officers stepped back toward their van, Scott looked up again, having some difficulty meeting her eyes.

"What are you doing here, Scott? Why have you been following me?"

He looked surprised that she knew she was being followed.

"I needed to talk to you. I moved to Las Vegas this past year—too cold in Atlantic City," he said, trying to smile. "I work at a wedding chapel," he added in embarrassment. "It pays the bills."

She had heard he was doing chapel weddings for a living, but hoped that he would be doing something else by now with his gifts for ministry, but only if he was healthy. She waited for him to continue with his story.

"Anyway, I've recently been in therapy. And now one of the things I've been doing is trying to make amends with some of the people I've hurt along the way—my family and some of the people I took advantage of. Of course, I can't, and shouldn't, contact everyone, but you were one of the ones I really felt I needed to talk to. You aren't in the phone book, so I decided I had to try to find you so I could say what I need to say. So, I'm saying it now. Jillian, I am so sorry for all the pain I caused you. I really did care for you. I know I really hurt you—and Marty. And I apologize. Will you forgive me?" he asked.

Jillian had spent the twelve years after Scott's removal from the clergy roster running from love. First, she took a new job in Madison at University Hospital. Then she turned down every opportunity she encountered that might lead to another hurt of the heart. She could barely even go to worship for a while—she, a former nurse missionary and parish nurse. She had never been so humiliated and hurt in her life. Not even Marty's father had damaged her heart as much as Scott had.

But now, here Jillian was, standing outside of her beautiful home, with her wonderful husband waiting for her inside. Suddenly, all those years of pain seemed to be worth every minute. If she had married Scott, there would be no John. The thought made her shudder.

And now, here was someone who had hurt her actually admitting it and asking for forgiveness. It seemed almost unreal, but good—very good.

"Of course I forgive you, Scott. I appreciate your apology, and I wish you well in your journey toward wellness," she said, and extended her hand to him.

He shook it, and smiled, revealing teeth that needed serious dental work. He looked ragged and worn, and very sad in general. But in that moment—just for a second—his eyes had a little bit of the light that they had had years before. It was amazing how much power those little words—*I'm sorry*—possess, for both the one saying them, and for the one hearing them. And it's equally empowering and healing to hear the words *I forgive you.*

"God bless you, Jillian," he said, then walked to his car door.

God already has, Scott. "You, too, Scott."

He turned the key. It took a couple of attempts for the old silver Buick to start, but finally the engine turned over. Jillian stepped toward the curb. Scott gave her a little wave, and she waved back, still not completely believing what had just happened.

Jillian approached the awaiting officers and explained the situation so they could write it up in their report and be on their way. She thanked them for their help and gave them each a tip for helping out, which seemed to change the attitude of the security guard with the gun, who had looked slightly disappointed at not getting to use it.

She walked back to her car, hit the code to open the gate, and drove up the circle drive to her home—their home. She had never felt so grateful.

Chapter Fourteen

Monica and Brent pulled themselves out of the Olympic-sized pool in their backyard simultaneously, almost like it was choreographed. They had been swimming laps together every day for the past two weeks, always racing each other on the final one.

Brent's doctor had suggested exercise as one helpful and healthy way to avoid his desire for alcohol. Monica was doing everything she could think of to help her son maintain sobriety. He had been going to AA meetings three times a week, had seen his own personal physician, and was beginning counseling with an AODA counselor named Kerri in two days. They said she was the best in the business, and Monica was pretty sure her son needed the best in the business.

Monica and Ben were also seeing a counselor. They wanted to stop enabling their son's habit and give him the best chance for recovery. They also wanted to make their own relationship as healthy as possible, for everyone's sake.

The two swimmers sat back on the warm cement, supporting themselves by their strong, lithe arms. Monica was more short of breath than her son, but that was to be expected. She had just turned fifty, but few people would ever suspect that by looking at her.

Brent turned to his mother with a serious look on his face. "I want to see her," he announced.

"See whom?" she asked.

"The girl."

"What girl?"

"The one I hit."

"Oh, honey, I don't think..."

"I *need* to see her, Mom," he said.

Monica shook her head in apprehension, but finally spoke. "I'll call Ms. Taylor and see what she says," Monica replied, sensing that her son would not be dropping this idea on his own anytime soon.

Ms. Stephanie "Steph" Taylor was Brent's lawyer. Monica felt she was a bit on the young side for such a huge case, but she came highly recommended. And whenever Monica or Ben mentioned who was representing Brent, they seemed to all agree that he was in good hands. Phrases like "go-getter," "up-and-coming," and "legal genius" were often used when people spoke of "Steph," as most people referred to her.

Monica grabbed a towel and sat on a chair near the pool to call this "wonder woman of the courtroom," as one acquaintance had called her. Monica certainly hoped she was. They needed a super-powered hero in this case. Court was in two weeks, and the entire family was on pins and needles.

Steph said she would speak with the girl's family. She didn't know if they would agree to it, but it could really be a good move for him to visit her. It would make "good press," she said. At that, Monica halted her. She had "had it," and then some, with the press.

"No press—at all—or it's off the table," Monica heard herself saying.

"As you wish, Ms. Morgan," the lawyer wisely answered.

Very early the next morning, Steph Taylor and a hospital employee accompanied Brent and Monica in a "staff-only" elevator. The doors opened, and they emerged quietly onto the sixth floor.

Monica hated the smell of hospitals. She really didn't like anything about them, actually, which was ironic since she had portrayed a heart surgeon for so many years. Even pretending to be a surgeon sometimes made her feel queasy. She truly had to do some legitimately fine acting on *O.R.,* considering her feelings on the subject. She was grateful for those years, however. The show had taken her to an entirely new level of stardom and made her financially secure for life, thanks to careful investing and residuals from the show over the years. It was still airing on some satellite networks and internet venues.

As they approached the hall leading to the girl's room, Monica wished she had not come. What would she say to these parents? She knew what she would want to say to someone who ran over one of her children while driving drunk. They turned into a small family room off the hallway. There sat a man and a girl of about sixteen, both who glared at Brent. The man was the father of the injured girl, Hannah. The girl sitting in the chair was Hannah's younger sister, Rachel.

Hannah's mother was in the hospital room with her daughter. The family members took turns holding her hand, talking to her, and reading to her. She was currently in a coma. The doctors had put her into it shortly after the accident, when her brain was swelling. It wasn't an uncommon practice. What was uncommon was for a person not to come out of it when they were supposed to. Hannah was breathing on her own, but could not seem to regain consciousness. The doctors had tried and tried, but Hannah would not wake up.

Her other injuries were healing, and the doctors were baffled as to why she was not coming out of her current state. They were going to try an experimental treatment in a few days if she didn't wake up, provided her parents gave them permission.

The nurse introduced them to one another. It was a very awkward situation, to say the least. After the introduction, Hannah's father led Brent down the hallway to another room, where Hannah's mother stood at Hannah's side, gently moving her limbs. The staff had been doing physical therapy with Hannah every day to make sure her muscles didn't atrophy. They had taught her parents some simple motions they could do with Hannah as well. Mrs. Thompson said it was especially important to Hannah, as she was an athlete—a runner. This would help her muscles stay strong. Now, all they needed was for her to wake up, she said, her voice breaking and tears clouding her eyes.

"We read to her every day. Her Bible," she said, pointing to a worn volume on a nightstand, "and other books. She is a voracious reader, and she had these books next to her bed at home when she was hit..." She stopped speaking, and looked directly at Brent. "Maybe you would like to spend some time with Hannah?" she asked. "You can read to her, if you run out of things to say."

Brent's eyes were burning. He just nodded without saying a word. Everyone else left and went back to the family room.

Brent looked at the young woman in the bed. Her cuts and bruises were almost gone. Her right leg was in a cast, though, which made him feel terrible, especially after hearing that she liked to run. He stepped closer to her, and was surprised when he found himself putting his hand on top of the young woman's hand.

It was soft and surprisingly warm. He looked at her face. There was a certain glow about it, almost angelic. He thought that she was one of the prettiest girls he had ever seen. He could sense also, in some strange way, the goodness emanating from her. He was entranced and couldn't stop looking at her.

Then he was jolted back into reality by the fact that he had put this beautiful, sweet, innocent person in this bed. He was the reason she was hooked up to monitors and an IV. He was the reason she wasn't reading her Bible and other books by herself. He felt awful, and his shoulders started to jerk rhythmically as he began to cry.

He looked at Hannah and squeezed her hand. "I'm so sorry, Hannah," was all that he could muster. He kept holding her hand and cried until the tears wouldn't come anymore. Finally, he released his grip and pulled a handful of tissues from a box on a portable tray table. He blew his nose—several rounds—then sat down in the chair Mrs. Thompson had vacated.

He tried to compose himself, and took several deep breaths. Then he looked at the stack of books and pulled one off the top of the pile. It was a book called *The Truth About Forever*. He read a chapter aloud. Then he glanced at the Bible.

He had never read a Bible. He'd never really seen a Bible, and certainly knew nothing about what was in it. He did know that it was a book by, and for, good people—and he wasn't one of them. He thought he shouldn't even touch it. Maybe if he came again another day—and came to the realization that he wanted to do that. He couldn't stay too long this time—his lawyer and Mom were waiting for him. But maybe he could come back tomorrow, if it was okay with the Thompson family.

He stood up, and wiped his nose one more time with a tissue. He was sure that he looked a mess, but he really didn't care.

"I hope I'll see you again, Hannah," he said, and touched her hand once more. "Again, I can't say it enough. I am so sorry that

Kathy J. Jacobson

I hurt you." He felt tears building again, so he quickly exited the room.

He stepped into the family room and was surprised by the quiet and steady conversation going on between the Thompsons and his mother. His mom wasn't usually the type for conversations with strangers. She wasn't really the type for conversations with much of anybody, actually. He just watched for a moment until he was noticed. They looked up at him then and stopped talking.

"I'll take my turn, hon," Mr. Thompson said to his wife, and Brent stepped out of the way for him to leave the room. He brushed past Brent and hurried down the hall. Brent wanted to say something to him, but he didn't have the words.

"I'm sorry if my husband seems rude. Hannah—she's Daddy's girl," Mrs. Thompson said quietly.

"I understand," Brent said, and Monica nodded. "Mrs. Thompson, may I come back to see Hannah tomorrow—about the same time, or any time you suggest? I can stay longer if I come back by myself. I could take a turn staying with Hannah and reading to her. I could give you and Mr. Thompson a break."

"I...guess that would be okay. We will try it one more time and see how it goes," she said.

"Thank you, ma'am," he said. "Is the same time okay?"

Mrs. Thompson nodded an okay. Rachel sat quietly, still looking coolly at Brent.

The three of them said goodbye, Monica extending her hand to Mrs. Thompson—another gesture which took Brent by surprise. Mrs. Thompson grasped onto Monica's hand like she was holding on for dear life, and it was clear that Monica was deeply moved. Afterward, they walked out of the room, not speaking a word.

True to his word, Brent returned early the next day. He read a few more chapters in the same book from the day before, beginning where the bookmark left off. After he closed the book, he glanced at the Bible on the stand, but again, he did not feel worthy of opening something that had the word "holy" on it. He was about as far from "holy" as it got, he thought to himself as he sat back.

He thought about the past seven years. That's when it all really began—when he really began drinking seriously—at a party thrown for him on his sixteenth birthday by friends in Bel Air. He had gotten a brand new sports car from his parents, as did Bart. Bart didn't do so badly with his—a few dings and scratches here and there—normal teen stuff—but it was a different story for Brent. A car was not a good gift for someone who liked to drink, who liked girls, and who liked to be reckless. The convertible was wrecked after six months, with many other "incidents" occurring in it, and with it, during that stretch of time, most of which his parents hadn't had a clue.

Brent was "punished" by not getting a replacement vehicle for an entire two months. He thought his parents were so mean. He now wished they had *never* replaced it. He suddenly felt so much older and wiser. He just wished he didn't always have to learn everything the hardest way possible.

Now he was probably going to go to prison—or jail at best. That was why he wanted to apologize to Hannah, before he couldn't. And what if she never woke up? That just couldn't be—a pretty, good girl like her. In fact, he could barely get her face out of his mind ever since he first saw it. There was something special about her—he just couldn't put it into words. She deserved to wake up. He looked at the ceiling in the room. *If you're really up there, help Hannah...and...help me.*

Brent went back to the hospital for a third day. Mr. Thompson still wouldn't speak to him. Mrs. Thompson said that the doctors were talking about doing that experimental treatment on Hannah the next day, since she was not able to wake up on her own or through their usual protocol. There were dangers involved, and they were all a bit on edge. But they were even more worried that if she didn't wake up soon, she wouldn't wake up at all.

Brent took his usual spot that morning at Hannah's side. He put his hand on hers and said hello to her. Again, he found himself just staring at her naturally pretty face. She was so different from the girls he knew. There was no makeup caked on her face, no black around her eyes making her look like a raccoon. She was just plain and simply—beautiful.

He sat down and started reading a chapter in the next book. The other one was finished now. He read a few chapters and then put it down. He looked at the nightstand. There was that Bible again. He looked at it, then looked away. He looked at it once more. He put his hand on it. So far, so good. No lightening bolts striking him dead—yet. He carefully put the book into his lap.

He noticed a number of bookmarks protruding from the volume. He didn't want to read the beginning. He never liked to start books at their beginning, for some reason. So, he looked at the biggest, most prominent bookmark, and opened to the page.

The top corner of the page had a name—"Luke." There were numbers on the page, too—lots of them. There was a big number "fifteen," and a smaller number, "eleven." Someone had highlighted some of the section and drawn a star near what appeared to be a title written in italics. Apparently, the story was called "*The Lost Son.*" He wondered why it earned a star, and began to read. "Then Jesus said, 'there was a man who had two sons...'"

Brent read the story out loud to Hannah, and as he did, tears began to roll down his cheeks. The Bible had some writing at the bottom of the page that helped the reader understand the story. It talked about how much God was like the father in the story, who had loved and forgiven one of his sons, even after he had done some pretty awful things. Brent looked surprised. Why had he never heard this before? He thought God—if there was one—was some perfect being who hated everyone who wasn't perfect. What was all this about forgiveness and love?

He closed the Bible gently and put it back in its spot. He thought that perhaps he should buy one—or download one onto his laptop when he got home. He would look into it first thing. He wanted to know more.

He looked at Hannah again. She looked so peaceful, but he didn't want her to look peaceful anymore. He found himself standing up.

He put his hand on hers again. Then, he gently moved his hand to her pretty face. He caressed the side of her face softly, like it would break if he touched it any harder.

"You are so beautiful, Hannah. Please wake up," he said.

She still slept on. He didn't know what possessed him, but he found his lips gently settling on hers. He kissed her softly, then stepped back. He looked toward the door, suddenly afraid. He thought that if Mr. Thompson had seen him do that, he might be a dead man.

Then he looked back at Hannah—and he practically fainted.

He pushed the nurse's button. Then he ran two doors down and across the hall to the family room. "Come quick!" he said to the Thompsons.

They stood up, a look of panic on their faces.

"What have you done now?" Mr. Thompson growled as he rushed past Brent, practically knocking him down.

Brent followed them. Then he heard Mr. Thompson's voice. "Oh, my Lord!"

Kathy J. Jacobson

Brent walked into the room, just as a nurse rushed in. The three Thompsons were around Hannah, who was frightened by all the monitors and tubes that were attached to her body, and not knowing where she was. The nurse talked calmly to her, explaining to her that she had been in an accident and was in the hospital. She paged the doctor and said that as soon as they got the okay, they would have Hannah off the machines.

Hannah gradually calmed down. She looked at her parents and sister, who were all crying tears of joy.

"I had the strangest dream," she said. "I was in heaven, but then came back to earth. There was a prince—at least I think he was a prince. He talked like a prince. He told me stories. He said he was sorry for something. He told me I was beautiful. He kissed me — and I woke up."

Just then Brent took a step closer to the bed. Mr. Thompson looked at him warily, but he was so happy about Hannah that nothing could completely wipe the smile off of his face.

Hannah noticed Brent, and looked at him quizzically. "Do I know you?" she asked quietly.

"Well—not really," Brent said.

Her eyes flashed when she heard his voice. "I do know you!" she exclaimed. "You're my prince!"

She smiled at him, and he felt like he was melting inside. He smiled shyly back at her and gently nodded his head.

The next day Brent arrived at the hospital at his usual time, but there was no Hannah.

"She is no longer a patient here," he was told by a nurse.

Of course, because of confidentiality laws, she could not tell him anything else. His countenance fell, and he felt lost. What would he do if he could never see Hannah again? The young woman had gotten under his skin. He had never looked forward to seeing anyone as much as he had looked forward to seeing Hannah, although he had to admit that he was a bit more nervous about seeing her now that she was conscious.

What would she say to him? Would she hate him for all that he had put her and her family through? His mind drifted back to the Bible story he had read at her bedside. If she really believed in God, perhaps she wouldn't hate him after all. It made him feel hopeful. In other ways, he wasn't sure he wanted to know what she had to say to him. He would find out, one way or the other, in court.

Court. It was right around the corner. He supposed that he should be happy that Hannah was going to live—and he was. In fact, it made him happier than he had ever been about anything in his life. It couldn't hurt his case, either, that she was awake, but that wasn't why he was happy. He was happy for Hannah. He couldn't explain just why, but he thought about her night and day, ever since the first moment he had laid eyes on her. He hopped into a taxi and looked out the window, looking back at the hospital where he had met her. *I hope she doesn't hate me.*

Ten days later, Brent, Monica, and Ben, all in sunglasses and hats, walked into the courthouse with Steph Taylor, making their way through a gauntlet of reporters. There were more flashbulbs going off than at the Oscars, Monica thought. The people called out nasty things to them as they walked by them, but they looked straight ahead, all but Brent, who looked at the sidewalk, feeling ashamed. The things the people were saying were mean. They were also true. He had a problem, and he knew it.

He hadn't heard from Hannah or the Thompsons since the day Hannah had awakened. He didn't even know how she was doing,

Kathy J. Jacobson

and hoped that he would at least hear some good news about her, even if he never got to see her again.

They entered the courtroom solemnly. Monica and Ben took seats in the first row, just behind Brent and Steph Taylor. There were few people there, as it was a closed session.

Brent glanced sideways to see if Hannah was at the other table, but she was not. Only her parents sat next to their lawyer. Brent was both disappointed and concerned. Had she experienced a setback? Was she okay?

He barely heard anything his lawyer said. She was saying something about him going to AA meetings, seeing a doctor, an AODA counselor—all part of his plan to overcome his addiction to alcohol. It had been agreed upon earlier that Brent's visits with Hannah would not be mentioned in the proceedings, as they might sway future jury members, if the case went to trial.

Hannah's attorney began to speak, but as he did, he was interrupted by Mr. Thompson.

"We don't want this young man punished. We want him to get help. Please, judge, let him get the help he needs."

Brent could barely believe what he was hearing. Mr. Thompson was asking for mercy on his behalf. Brent's eyes began to moisten.

The judge went on to say that he could not let a third offense of DUI, which had caused serious bodily injury, go completely unpunished. He said he would like to speak with both attorneys in his chambers.

Brent could tell that the Thompson's lawyer looked very unhappy. Most likely he was hoping for a big jury trial and a huge settlement of some sort, and Mr. Thompson was not helping him get that.

The proceeding recessed for an hour, and the Bastiens were shown to a small room, with a pitcher of water sitting on a small wooden table, with paper cups to the side.

They sat quietly, nervously sipping water and waiting for their lawyer to return. Monica was just going to say something when Steph Taylor walked into the room. She sat down and said she had a deal she thought they should consider.

The judge slammed the heavy wooden gavel and loudly proclaimed, "Next case."

Brent was led out of the courtroom by the bailiff. He looked at his mom and dad as he walked by, who were tearful and holding each other. He gave them a reassuring smile and told them he would call when he was allowed.

Brent was off to jail. He would be spending the next three months at the Beverly Hills jail facility. His family would pay for him to serve his time there rather than at the county jail. While incarcerated, he would continue to attend his three AA meetings per week and AODA counseling appointments. After his time was served, he would be on probation for eighteen months, and still have to attend his meetings and counseling if the counselor recommended further treatment. He was also assigned community service hours, was responsible for all of Hannah's medical bills, her attorney's fees, and a million dollars to Hannah for the pain and inconvenience he had caused her. The Thompsons had actually asked for less, but their lawyer had argued for more. The judge had settled somewhere in between.

Monica and Ben may have been crying, but they were mostly tears of happiness and relief. Considering the gravity of recent events, they felt that this was a far better outcome than they could have imagined. They also felt, for the first time, that their son had a chance of getting better. Brent had seemed different since this accident, and especially since he had met Hannah. Perhaps witnessing someone lying unconscious in a hospital bed because of one's own actions may well have done the trick.

Monica told Ben to wait a moment before they left the building. She wanted to call Jillian and tell her the news. Jillian had told her earlier that day that she would be praying for them, and Monica wanted to share their good news and thank her for her prayers. *Maybe there's actually something to this praying business.*

Saturday was visiting day at the jail. Ben, Monica, and Bart had all come to see Brent, bringing him some of his favorite magazines. They talked about Bart's play, which had just had its run extended. Brent was so grateful that he had been able to see the show with his parents while he was still on the outside, and was intensely proud of his twin brother.

Brent couldn't believe how much he missed his family. He also missed the sun and the pool. When he had been at home, he had felt like he was getting into shape again, for the first time in a long time. He had forgotten how great it felt to be physically fit. They had an exercise area at the jail, but it was pretty small. He did his best, however, to try to take advantage of it. Any time he thought about complaining, he would make himself think about the alternatives, which were very sobering thoughts.

His mom looked better today. He had been very worried about her. He felt terrible about what he had put his own family through. It was almost as bad as what he had done to Hannah and her family. He tried not to get too down on himself, however. With the help of his counselor, he realized that whenever he got really negative, that was when he started to think about alcohol. It had such a wonderful, yet short-lived, numbing effect. The problem came when that effect wore off. Then he would take the next drink...and the next...and the next.

Brent hugged his parents and brother goodbye and had just

returned to his room when he heard someone saying, "Bastien, you've got another visitor."

"Who could it be?" he wondered. The only people who cared about him in the world had just left. Maybe his lawyer needed to speak with him.

He walked around the corner. The guard was pointing at a table where a person was sitting. There sat the most beautiful young woman. It took him a moment to completely comprehend who it was. It was Hannah!

He had thought she was pretty when she was unconscious, wearing a hospital gown, pale-faced and recovering from bruises and cuts, her hair unwashed and not completely combed for weeks while in a hospital bed. She had had a special glow, however, and he had thought she was pretty, even in her former state. But now she was dazzling. Her beautiful chestnut-colored hair was full-bodied and fell onto her shoulders, gleaming. Her blue-green eyes looked happy, and her cheeks were rosy. And when she smiled at him he nearly tripped over his own feet.

He walked to the table. "Hannah?" he asked, just to make sure.

"Yes, it's me," she said.

He pulled out the chair and looked at her. He couldn't stop staring.

"How have you been?" he asked. "I was so worried when you weren't in court."

"I was just finishing up my last day at the rehab center that day. I wanted to be there, but I had to complete my stay. Another patient was moving into my room the next day. I'm doing some physical therapy at home now, and will go to outpatient rehab when the cast comes off," she said, glancing down at her right leg, which he hadn't even noticed.

Brent felt like he was under some sort of spell, but seeing the cast brought him back to reality.

"I'm so sorry, Hannah. I have a problem. But I'm working on it," he said, his eyes starting to smart.

Then she reached across and put her hand on top of his. His hand began to tingle.

"I know you do. That's why I asked my parents not to hurt you, but to help you," she said, her hand still on his. It reminded him of the hospital, when he would put his hand on hers. He wondered if she had been able to feel it somehow.

"Visiting hours end in five minutes!" a voice shouted out.

She moved her hand from his. He wanted to grab it and kiss it, but he didn't dare. He watched her reach down onto her lap and lift something from it.

"I brought you something," she said.

It was a Bible, similar to the one he had read from on the night-stand in her hospital room. She put it down on the table in front of him.

"Thank you, Hannah. That was so kind of you. And you coming here today—that was very kind of you, too." He paused a moment. "Why did you come?" he asked softly.

Hannah turned the Bible back toward herself. She turned to a spot near the back of the book and took a bookmark from the front of the book and put it in a page. "Read Matthew chapter twenty-five, starting at verse thirty-one. That's part of the reason," she said, closing the Bible and turning it back around and pushing it toward him.

She stood up from the table, grabbing a crutch from the floor on her right side and putting it under her right armpit.

Brent stood up when she did. He wanted to touch her. Instead, he picked up the Bible and looked at her. Finally he got up the nerve to ask. "What was the other part of the reason?"

"You're my prince," she said matter-of-factly, then smiled at him and turned to leave.

Brent stared after her as a guard held the door for her on the way out. Other visitors were standing and leaving the room, too. He realized that his mouth was hanging open, and he quickly shut it. He wanted to run after her and hold her. He wanted to tell her... he wasn't sure what he wanted to tell her. He only knew that he had never felt like this before in his entire life. And it was a good feeling. A very good feeling.

Chapter Fifteen

Darius dragged himself out of bed. It was Sunday morning. At least there were no chores this morning because of church. He looked in the mirror as he got ready to step into the shower stall. He noticed something. The muscles on his arms and shoulders looked bigger, and his face looked different, too. His cheeks were filled out, and he had a healthy, athletic look about him.

How could so much change in just three weeks? Miss Nancy sure knew how to cook. He supposed that had something to do with it. He thought back to his home—if you could call it that—after his grandmother's death. She had rented a small house and she was a great cook, like Nancy. After her death, he lived with his aunt in her tiny apartment and slept on the couch. There was never anything to eat in the refrigerator. Sometimes there were some cans of beer. He tried one once when he was thirteen, and his aunt's boyfriend nearly beat him to a pulp.

He relied mostly on the school-provided breakfasts and lunches for his meals. He hated the summertime, especially the first and last two weeks of vacation when there was no summer school. There were some very hungry days during those periods of time.

Darius had one more semester of high school to complete. He had purposely blown a test so he would have to repeat a class and come back. He wondered what he would do for food after that. Maybe prison wouldn't be so bad after all, if you got fed. But the thought of being in prison with some of the people he knew were there, frightened him. He always acted tough on the streets, but inside he felt like he always had—like a frightened and trapped kid, with nowhere else to go, and no way out.

He stepped into the hot, steamy shower. He closed his eyes, loving the feeling of the water streaming down his back. He had taken more showers in the last few weeks than in the last few years. The water didn't even heat up in his aunt's apartment until you were almost done getting washed up. And if her boyfriend got in there first—well, forget about there being any warm water left.

Darius toweled off with the softest towel to ever touch his skin, and put on his crisp, white dress shirt. He had never owned such a nice shirt before, or any pants like the black dress slacks, which he now decided weren't so bad after all. He didn't like the style of the shoes, but they were new. Everything was *new*—his clothes, food, a huge bed to himself in his own room, a shower with hot water, getting up before the sun, and *never-ending* chores.

He went downstairs where he smelled eggs, potatoes, and bacon frying. He entered the kitchen where Buck was dishing up a plate of food for Nancy. Buck had made breakfast this morning, giving Nancy a break as she did most of the cooking during the week.

"Mornin', Darius," Buck said.

Darius mumbled a good morning back. For some reason, it was still difficult for him to show any emotion, especially anything positive, toward Buck. He slid into his chair and gave a muffled thank-you as Buck placed a plate full of food in front of him. He tried not to act too anxious to eat it, but he knew he would probably wolf down the delicious fare after the table prayer. He loved the fried potatoes, especially. They reminded him of his younger years living with his grandma. He sure did miss her. He had thought more about her in the past three weeks than he had in a long time. He thought it was because of going to church. She was a good churchwoman, like Miss Nancy.

After Buck dished up his own plate of food, he sat down, and Buck and Nancy said the table prayer. "Come, Lord Jesus, be our guest, and let these gifts to us be blessed. Blessed be God who is our bread; may all the world be clothed and fed." Darius bowed his head during the prayer. He knew the words by now, but he just couldn't get them past his lips. Then he proceeded, despite his best efforts, to quickly devour his breakfast.

That morning in church Darius' ears perked up when he heard his name. Not really *his* name, but someone in the Bible named Darius—King Darius. A man was up in the front of the church reading a lesson from the book of Daniel. From the sound of it, this King Darius was a bad guy, or at best, a fool. *Figures*, Darius thought to himself.

But then Pastor Jim went on to talk about both the saving of Daniel from the lions' den, and of King Darius. He said that Darius came to know and recognize the God of Daniel, and was a changed man. He mentioned that by the end of the scripture, it said that Darius had "received the kingdom." Pastor Jim said that might have been referring to an earthly kingdom, but he also thought it could have meant a heavenly one as well.

After the service, Darius stood in the narthex with Buck and Nancy, looking shyly down at the ground. Buck and Nancy's many friends came up and said hello. He mumbled a hello back to each of them. Then Pastor's Jim's wife and two little boys came over, along with Rick, who now almost always sat with them.

"Darius!" one of the twins shouted. Darius could never seem to keep their names straight—they both looked exactly alike to him. "You're famous! You were in the Bible story! I'm glad you stopped being so mean," Matt said innocently.

Janet, the boy's mother, told her son that this wasn't the same Darius, it was just the same name. She looked apologetically at Darius. "I'm sorry," she said.

"It's okay," he replied quietly. But he had to admit to himself later, the words rang in his ears the rest of the day.

After a huge Sunday dinner at noon, they rested for half an hour, then went out to work on a project in the steer barn. Most of the cattle were out grazing, but a few were inside who had had some health issues the past week. Darius had never known there was so much to learn and know about animals. They were always getting diseases or had some other sort of problem. The vet came out at least once a week, and the rest of the time Buck or the other workers had to administer medicines of some sort to either prevent or treat a malady.

Buck asked Darius to get a bucket for him from an area next to one of the recovering animals. Darius was feeling lazy—and a bit scared of the huge animal, he hated to admit—and hesitated a moment.

"Never mind. I'll get it myself," Buck said and walked over to pick up the metal pail.

For some reason, the steer was startled by Buck's presence. It reared its head to one side and then the other. When it did, it smacked Buck right in the side of his chest, and down to the cement floor he went. Then, to make matters worse, the heavy animal stepped on his arm.

Darius didn't know what to do at first, but he couldn't just stand there. He rushed to Buck, took him by the arm that was not injured and pulled him away from the animal, who was tied up, thankfully.

Darius could not speak. He had never seen Buck look like he did right then. This was the strong man who had pinned him to the ground when he tried to take his wallet and watch. Buck was not attempting to get up. His face was ashen, and he was holding his side.

"I think you'd better get Miss Nancy," Buck said in a weak voice.

Darius ran faster than he had ever run in his life. He felt like crying for some reason. He was also mad—mad at himself for not getting that bucket and for being afraid. Now Buck was hurt. The one man on earth who actually cared...

The door to the kitchen slammed open as he entered. He called for Nancy, over and over, panic setting in. He finally found her upstairs just waking up from a little nap. She took one look at Darius' face and knew that something was very wrong. He told her what had happened. She quickly descended the stairs with him, holding onto the rail. She felt faint. She had lost one husband...she couldn't lose another.

When they reached the bottom of the stairs, Nancy walked as calmly as she could to the telephone and called 9-1-1. She was pretty sure from Darius' description that it would be best to have Buck checked out, even though she knew he would have a fit about it.

She asked Darius to hold her arm as they walked to the barn, as she felt unsteady. Buck was still in the same position and still holding his side. Blood was coming through his shirt sleeve from where the steer had put its weight and broken the skin.

"Hi, darlin'," he said to Nancy. "Got myself into a bit of a predicament," he tried to joke, but winced as he said it. His breathing sounded raspy. "Pretty sure I've got a broken rib or two."

"Sit tight. Help is on the way," Nancy said, kneeling down at his side, removing his hat, which was askew on his head, and stroking the side of his face. She was so relieved that he was talking. She wanted to cry, but forced herself to be strong. They could hear a siren wailing in the distance.

"I will," he said, trying to smile.

Darius felt awful. He wanted to run away, but where would he go? And if he ran away, he would end up in prison for certain. He just stood and stared at the sight, trying with all of his might not to act as terrified as he felt inside. Finally, the ambulance pulled into the driveway. Darius stepped outside of the barn and waved to the driver, then two paramedics rushed to the scene.

Buck had guessed right. He had broken ribs, four of them. He also had a hairline fracture in his arm and a laceration that required stitches. Buck mentioned that he could add that to his "collection" of scars from over the years.

Darius sat with Nancy while they took Buck for X-rays. She could tell the young man was upset and tried to calm him by saying that Buck was a strong man and had been through a lot worse than this in his life.

Darius didn't know what possessed him, but he snorted when she said that. He was sure Buck received many bumps and scratches working on the farm, but it wasn't like he lived in Darius' neighborhood. And thinking of the house at the ranch, he figured that Buck had been raised with a "silver spoon" in his mouth.

Now Nancy was one of the kindest, most patient people one could ever meet, but when Darius made that noise, she lit into him.

"You don't think Buck's had tough times, do you, Darius?" she said in an unusually angry tone. "Let me tell you a few things, young man."

For the next fifteen minutes, she gave Darius the condensed

version of Buck's childhood. He had grown up in Texas. His dad worked the oil rigs and was rarely home. When he was at home, he was usually drunk, and when he drank, he was abusive. She said that some of the scars to which Buck was referring were cigarette burns and cuts he sustained at the hands of his father.

Nancy said that Buck's mother was a frail and scared woman, not knowing how to stop her husband, and when she did try, he turned his fury on her. She unfortunately continued on in the relationship until she ended up in a coma. She was never the same again after she came out of it. Buck's father went to prison for a short time, then after he was released, went back to the oil rigs. He died in an explosion and fire on one of them. Buck's mother ended up in a nursing facility. Buck was put into foster care and proceeded to run away.

He was fifteen. The pastor in town, Pastor Leroy Swenson, and his wife, Susan, took Buck in after he had been apprehended by one of his parishioners, who was a county sheriff's deputy. Buck was angry and uncooperative. Pastor Leroy wasn't one for giving up, but even he didn't know quite what to do with this young "buck," and he often mentioned that Buck was appropriately named. Pastor Leroy and Susan were at the end of their ropes, when Pastor Leroy's brother, Jack, stepped in. He had met Buck at church and suggested that maybe the boy needed some fresh air and to learn about hard work. He made the offer to have Buck come out to his ranch and stay there for a week or two. If nothing else, Leroy and Susan could have a little break.

Buck fell in love with life on the ranch—after he got through the shock of the first few days. By the end of his time there, he refused to leave. Jack said he didn't mind if he stayed, as long as he did his work, was respectful to all the adults in his life, and went to school and to church on Sunday. Buck stayed. Buck always said that the Swensons—all of them—saved his life.

Darius felt so ashamed. He had assumed that Buck was just some wealthy person who never had a bad day in his life. Now he really had to fight back tears. Not only did he feel awful about Buck, but he made Nancy, who was the nicest woman he had ever known next to his grandma, upset. He felt like a heel. When Nancy went up to the nurse's station to speak with one of them, a tear rolled down his cheek. Darius wiped it away quickly, before anyone could see.

They got home in the evening, just as the sun was setting. The dogs were ecstatic to see them, and Darius held onto their collars so they wouldn't jump up on the ailing Buck. One of them was his favorite—"Jack," who Darius now realized must have been named for the rancher with whom Buck had lived. The weekend foreman and hired hands were all pitching in to do extra work, and told Nancy that Darius could meet with the weekday foreman the next morning after breakfast. He would assign him some chores to do throughout the day.

Nancy had spoken with Jillian on the phone, telling her what had happened and asking for advice. Jillian had been honest with her, that Buck would experience a lot of pain, especially over the first three weeks. Broken ribs were one of the most obnoxious injuries. One can't "set" them. Often it takes three to six weeks to heal, possibly more, depending on one's age and general health. Sleeping would be the most difficult challenge in those early weeks, and she suggested they find a way to keep him as still as possible, either propped up in bed or in a recliner. Buck had been given some powerful pain meds, which would help to some extent. Jillian told Nancy to make sure he "stayed ahead of the pain."

Darius was very quiet when they returned to the ranch house. He had no idea what to say to Buck. He could barely even look his way. He was also very afraid that this would mean he would be sent to prison. Darius thought he would have to leave this place, and suddenly realized he didn't want to leave. That made him even more scared, because he actually liked the ranch. He actually liked these people. It was dangerous to like places and people, because they could be taken away from you in an instant.

Buck decided that his favorite chair, surrounded on all sides with soft pillows, would be the best place to spend his first night home. He wasn't used to being pampered. He wasn't used to feeling pain, at least not as an adult. He was a big, strong man, and it was killing him to have to move so gingerly and have people doing things for him. But he had no choice. Every little movement was excruciating. He had coughed once, and thought he was going to go through the roof. He guessed that Jillian had been right about managing the pain, and succumbed to taking one of the painkillers from its container on the end table next to his chair, swallowing it without water.

Darius tiptoed through the room on his way to the staircase to the bedrooms. He didn't know what to say, and hoped he wouldn't be seen and could avoid a conversation. But Buck saw him out of the corner of his eye and called to him.

"Darius," he said in a firm, but gentle tone.

Darius turned, his foot on the bottom step. "Yes, sir." It was the first time he had ever spoken to Buck in such a respectful way.

"Come here a minute," Buck said, and tried to sit up taller, grimacing in pain.

Darius walked over and stood in front of him, his head hanging in shame. He felt it was because of him that Buck was in this chair and so uncomfortable.

"Darius, do you like it here?"

Darius thought Buck was going to suggest that he go back to jail the next morning, and words would just not come out of his mouth. He stood like a statue, not knowing what to say or do. He was afraid that if he spoke, he might begin to cry.

Buck watched the young man's face and knew that he was struggling. "You don't have to answer me now, but if you want to, you can stay here as long as you would like, if the judge agrees," Buck said.

That was the last thing Darius imagined Buck would say. His eyes were smarting. He had to get out of this room. He simply nodded his head slightly. He started to move toward the stairs, then turned around.

"I'm sorry," he said so quietly Buck could barely hear him.

"'Nothing to be sorry 'bout. Stuff like this happens all the time on a ranch."

Darius couldn't find any words again. He wasn't used to being shown such mercy. Again, he just nodded his head and then headed for the steps.

"G'night, son," Buck said.

The first time Buck had called him "son," Darius had jumped down his throat.

"Good night," Darius said, and ran up the steps as quickly as he could.

Chapter Sixteen

Greta and Drew walked out of the counselor's office hand-in-hand. The past few weeks had been among the most challenging in their lives, and in their relationship. The good news was that both of them agreed on one thing that morning—that their marriage, and their love for one another, felt stronger than ever.

They walked to their vehicles quietly, thinking about the session with the psychologist, Ms. Young. She certainly knew how to get them talking, expressing feelings they had never shared with anyone before. It was a very cleansing experience.

They had parked next to one another, Drew in his Mercedes SUV, Greta in her fifteen-year-old compact car that she insisted on keeping until it "dropped." At first, Drew had wanted to replace it, but he had come to admire Greta's ethics about not just throwing out everything because it wasn't the newest or nicest, or buying something just because it was the trend or impressive.

They stopped at the rear of the cars. Drew pulled her into a strong embrace. He drew back slightly and looked down at Greta adoringly.

"I wish I didn't have to go back to work," he said, his eyes looking deeply into hers.

"I wish I didn't have to go the university, but the dean of the department wants to take me to lunch and then on a walking tour of campus," she replied. "I am excited, though, I will admit."

"And you should be," he told her, stroking her face. "How about a kiss to get me through the rest of the day?"

Greta gave him a kiss she thought would fit the bill. She loved being married to Drew.

"How's that?" she asked, when she stepped back.

"I think that will do," he said, breathless, and pulled her even closer.

"I'd better go," Greta said.

"Yes, you'd better," Drew agreed.

She smiled and pecked him on the cheek, then climbed into her ancient carriage.

The on-campus lunch with the dean was surprisingly delicious, and the conversation was exhilarating. Greta felt like she was going to enjoy her work if the dean was any indication of the entire department. She had briefly met some of the staff during the interview process, and they had seemed very nice, so that was a good start. They walked through the art wing of the fine arts building once more, then walked across a beautifully groomed green.

One area on the other side was under construction, with two bulldozers and a backhoe getting the plot ready for some type of major project.

"What's going on here?" Greta asked as they walked by the workers. She couldn't remember what had been there when she interviewed.

"There used to be an old academic building there from the

Kathy J. Jacobson

1960s. We took it down and are starting to build our new early childhood and learning center. It will house the academic program in that field and will be state-of-the-art. It will also host an on-campus daycare, for the children of faculty, staff, and students. We want to make this a family-friendly campus, while developing top-notch early childhood teachers and behavioral scientists. It will be done sometime next spring, and we will begin taking applications for the fall at that time," the dean proudly announced.

Greta stopped walking for a moment.

"Are you okay?" the dean asked.

"Yes...I am," she said. She suddenly felt different. She felt like this was some sort of sign. Greta couldn't wait to get home and talk to Drew.

Drew came home around seven, weary from a long afternoon of meetings. He was happily surprised when he walked into the house. Music was playing—for the first time in weeks. He could hear noise coming from the kitchen and Greta humming along with a song as she worked on the finishing touches of their dinner.

He watched her from the doorway for a moment, then quietly walked up behind her, sliding his arms around her. "I take it you had a nice afternoon," he said into her ear.

She turned around and faced him. "Yes, but not as nice as I am hoping my evening will be," she said, and kissed him.

"What went on at that campus?" he asked, smiling.

"I'll tell you over dinner," she said, her fingers untying his tie. "Let's eat—I have a lot to talk to you about."

Over their spicy lentils and vegetables, Greta told him about how impressed she was again with the campus and the art program. Then she moved on to the subject of the new construction on the green. She excitedly shared the news about the early childhood center, then a more serious look crossed her face. Greta sat quietly for a moment, and took a big breath before continuing.

"Drew, there's something I'd like you to think about. I think this fall we should start trying—for a baby. He or she could be born in the summer, hopefully, then go to the center while I'm at work when the fall semester begins. The dean said parents will be encouraged to stop in and eat lunch with their children, read a book to them, or just visit when they have a free period. If they are infants, parents get to hold them and feed them. The school wants it to be a family-friendly environment. I felt—I felt like it was a sign from above when I saw those bulldozers. They were tearing down the past and building something new...sort of like us. What do you think?" she said, her green eyes flashing.

"I think I love that idea—almost as much as I love you," he told her. His eyes were brimming as he reached across the table for her hand. He knew the counselor and support group were helping. And he had never prayed as hard for anyone as he had prayed for Greta over the past few weeks. He smiled as Greta got up from her chair and sat down on his lap, ready to kiss him. Drew felt at that moment that they were beginning to get their lives back, and that they were going to be better than ever.

Tommy watched Maria as she slept. Things were slowly but surely returning to normalcy in the house. He and Alison had gone car shopping the day before. She was a bit hesitant at first, and had mentioned that maybe she should wait to get her license. Tommy could tell that she was frightened, and told her that the sooner she got "back in the saddle," the better. In fact, he made her drive to and from the car lot in his nice car.

Alison was visibly shaking for the first few miles behind the wheel, but as she and her dad began talking about school and

Kathy J. Jacobson

their summer plans, she became more calm and relaxed. When they arrived at the lot, they were pleased to find a car that was one year newer than the one that had been totaled in the accident, in a different color. Alison wanted as few reminders of the previous car as possible, although they agreed that had it not been so well-made, both Alison and Maria might have been injured far worse than either of them had been. Thus, they picked the same make and model. They also felt committed to buying from the manufacturer Tommy's father and grandfather had worked for, for many, many years.

The car would be dropped off at their home, as Alison didn't have her license to drive it home yet. It would stay in the garage until Maria was given the okay to drive again or be a licensed driver in the vehicle to ride along with her daughter, or Alison got her license, whichever happened first.

Maria turned over and looked into Tommy's eyes. He kissed her gently and moved closer to her. He kissed her again.

"Tommy," Maria said, and pulled him closer. Just then she felt a bit of pain as her stitches and staples stretched, and she stopped, a look of discomfort crossing her face. "I guess I'll have to get rid of these staples first," she said apologetically, her hand stroking his cheek.

He kissed her gently, then nodded understandingly. He wished he did not have to go to work. The day before had been his first day back. A few people asked about Maria, but mostly it was right back to business. He wondered what had happened to the company and people he had once worked with. When the chairman of the board had retired two years prior, things slowly and subtly began to change, and not for the better. People used to be the priority in the firm. Now, projects and profits seemed to rule the day.

Amanda Richards had been cold and business-like upon his return. He didn't really mind. It was an improvement over her previous unprofessional behavior. It still bothered him that he had gone right along with it, though. He wondered how long it would take him to forgive himself, if that was even possible.

Tommy forced himself out of the bed to get ready for the day. He didn't used to feel like that—ever. It used to be a joy to go to work. Now it felt like drudgery to go to the office.

The day dragged on and on for Tommy. All he wanted to do was be at home with Maria. He had called her twice already, just to make sure that she was okay. A neighbor was going to check in on her, too, and a visiting nurse was coming over at two o'clock. Maria was getting stronger every day and following the doctor's instructions impeccably. She hated lying around, and he knew she was worried about the deli. It would help after she hired a business manager, but now that had been put on hold because of the accident.

Tommy sighed as he sat at his desk, looking over papers for a project he just didn't really care about anymore. Maybe he should start looking for a new position. Something closer to home. He was tired of driving in the heavy traffic toward the city every morning, and really didn't care for taking the crowded train. He wondered if there was some opportunity right in Libertyville. He hadn't looked at the employment section of a newspaper since he was a teen. He had worked for this company ever since a summer internship be-tween his junior and senior years of college. He was offered a posi-tion with them before he even graduated and had been working for them ever since, advancing in the ranks throughout the years. It suddenly made him feel old, being at the same place for so long. He felt like he needed a new adventure.

Thinking of adventures made him think of Jillian, and her move west to begin a new phase in her life. She had quit a good

Kathy J. Jacobson

job to fulfill her dream of becoming a writer, and she had done it. And now she was doing even more new things—screenwriting, directing, and consulting—working with John. Suddenly, John's words about working with Jillian, and how he never got tired of being with his wife, rang in Tommy's ears. *That's it.* Tommy put his papers in his briefcase, closed it, picked up his jacket, and went home for the day, right at the close of normal work hours. He was not putting in any extra time today. He wanted to go home to his wife.

Maria was sitting on the couch, deep in thought when Tommy arrived home. She was thinking about how crazy this past year had been. She loved her business, but she loved her family even more. She was beginning to have second thoughts about whether it was such a good idea after all, when Tommy came excitedly into the room, home earlier than he had been in ages.

He sat down next to her and gave her a kiss. "You look very serious. Are you feeling all right?" he asked, touching her soft curls.

"I was just thinking that maybe I should sell the deli," she said, taking him by surprise.

"What? Maria, you love that deli!"

"I do, but I love you more," she responded sincerely.

He looked moved, but continued. "That's great to hear, but I was just thinking that maybe it's time for me to consider a new job," he said.

"A new job?" Maria asked, a bit stunned by the idea. "Do you have any ideas about what you would do, or where you would like to work?"

"Well, I did have one idea, but it won't work out if my possible boss would sell her business," he said.

Maria looked at him quizzically.

"You are looking for a business manager, aren't you? And one who understands your work, who is a hard worker, and who wouldn't mind doing some extra duties when needed..."

"Tommy, are you serious? Could we afford it?"

"Yes, I'm serious. I want to work for you, and with you, Maria. I miss you too much. I need you. And can we afford it? I think so. We might have to do some figuring, and maybe make a few life-style changes, but I think we could make it work. What do you think about that idea?"

Maria's eyes were shining. "You're hired," she said softly, then kissed him.

Tommy went to Mr. Francis' office the next morning to give his notice. He also informed him that he was taking a few hours off to take Maria to her medical appointment, then would be taking the vacation time he had coming beginning the next week. Mr. Francis didn't even try that hard to talk him out of it, which was a bit hard to take. But Tommy knew that Mr. Francis was grooming Amanda for big things in the firm, and she would be very happy to take over Tommy's office, he was certain.

He also thought that he saw Mr. Francis, a married man of many years, looking at Amanda, and her at him, in a way that suggested there may have been more than just work going on after hours in the past week or so while Tommy had been absent. That made him feel sad, but also made him feel even more certain that he was making the right decision.

Tommy held the door open for Maria when they got home from the appointment. Alison had just come home from school. She was busily gathering up books and materials to go over to a friend's house for a final project they were working on in their physics course. Maria gave her a container of homemade granola bars to take along.

Tommy and Maria saw her off at the door, Alison giving them both a quick peck on the cheek as she rushed by, a backpack slung over one shoulder. Her friend—a new driver—and the girl's mom were waiting for her in a car parked in the driveway, its engine running.

When she reached the car, Alison turned and smiled at them, waving goodbye with her one free hand. They waved back, smiling and enjoying the fact that Alison finally seemed more like herself. It helped that Maria was doing so much better. Alison could see her improvement each day, and felt more and more confident that her mom would make a full recovery. It also helped that she knew John Anthony would soon be home for almost a month. Alison was so looking forward to that—almost as much as they were.

Maria shut the door as the car drove away, and rested her back against it. She reached out for Tommy. It scared him. He thought she was having some type of problem, until she pulled him close, and looked lovingly into his face.

"My stitches and staples are out," she said, her lips curling into a smile.

"Maria..."

Chapter Seventeen

Brent found himself counting the minutes to the next visiting day. He didn't know if Hannah would return, but something inside of him felt hopeful. Never had he thought about someone like he thought about Hannah. Every time he went into the activity room, which was the room used for visits, he saw her face. When he woke up first thing in the morning, it was there as well. At night, he couldn't get to sleep as he thought of her smile, and her words "because you're my prince."

He didn't feel like a prince. The more he sat and thought about what he had done, the worse he felt. He wanted to do something that would help him become a person who deserved such a title of respect. He wanted to be a man that Hannah could...he wouldn't let himself finish the thought. What would a woman like Hannah want with someone like him?

Hannah's parents had mentioned at the hospital that she was studying at a small Christian university in the area. In the fall, she would begin her final year in the social work program. He thought that was a fitting major for someone with a heart like hers. Few people would come to visit the person who hit them with a car, putting them in the hospital for a month and into a cast and physical therapy for even longer.

He decided that when he got his chance to use the jail computer that afternoon, he was going to look up her school online. It would make him feel closer to her somehow, if he knew more about her world. Thinking of Hannah and her world made him turn to the Bible she had given him.

He had been reading some of it every night. The bookmark that was in it was very helpful. It was blue and satin-like, and was long and wide. In the left-hand column was a heading with words and phrases below it. The heading said: "When you feel..." Across from it was a heading for the right-hand column, which said: "Read this passage." Under that column were Bible passages that corresponded to the feeling.

There were also some reading plans listed in the back of the Bible, but he thought he would stick to the bookmark first. Hannah had put it in there, so he wanted to say that he had read all of the passages on it. He found himself coming back to some of them more than once. He found that when he read them, he felt something new in his heart—hope.

Brent still had to use the table of contents to find each scripture passage, and wished he had his laptop to help him learn how to pronounce some of those crazy names. There were some easy ones—Daniel, Ruth, Matthew, Mark, Luke, and John. But some of them—wow! The Bible Hannah had given him said it was a "Study Bible." At the bottom of each page, there were explanations of the writing above it. He was very grateful for that, as it did seem to help. Sometimes the commentary would direct him to another spot in the book, and he would read that, too.

He didn't want to get too sidetracked, however. He hoped to have read all the ones on the bookmark before Saturday. He read the name of the next one in line and laid back on his small bed that was bolted into the wall, and got down to business. The passage was from a book he had been reading in before, and he was proud when he found it without looking at the table of contents. He thought that Hannah would like that, too, and he smiled to himself as he began to read.

Saturday visiting hours came and went—and no Hannah. His parents had come early again. He felt bad because all he could think about was Hannah while they were visiting. After they had gone, he watched the door. He had read all the passages on the bookmark, and wanted to tell Hannah and thank her again for the gift. Finally the guard called out that visiting hours would be over in five minutes.

He gave up hope and sadly went back to his room. It was difficult to mask his disappointment, and suddenly he was glad he was not on the outside at that moment. He wanted a drink. Having a drink was his usual way of dealing with anything that made him unhappy, and not seeing Hannah definitely made him feel unhappy. He plopped down on the bed, which was not a good idea. The foam pad was a far cry from his plush bed at home. He sighed and closed his eyes, and found himself talking out loud. He realized at that moment that for the first time in his life—he was praying.

The mail came to the jail on Monday morning. Brent had never received a piece of mail before, and was curious when they called his name. He thought perhaps it was something from his lawyer, or Hannah's attorney. Hannah. He couldn't get her out of his mind, no matter how hard he tried. *You don't deserve someone like Hannah, anyway.* That was what Brent told himself.

He looked at the envelope the jailer had handed him. It didn't look like business mail. It looked like a card of some type. It had a return address on it he did not recognize. It had been opened, but he knew it would be.

He sat down on a chair to read it. He pulled out a note card that had an ocean scene on it. He opened it slowly, wondering what it was about. His eyes jumped to the bottom of the page, where it was signed simply as "Hannah."

He wasn't sure he wanted to read it. Was this one of those "it was nice knowing you" letters? He certainly wouldn't blame her if it was. But still, she had given him a Bible. She had come to visit him. She had called him her prince. He forced himself to start at the beginning.

Dear Brent,

I hope this note gets to you by Saturday morning. I forgot to tell you that we have a family wedding this Saturday...

Hannah had been out of town! She couldn't call him or text him to tell him, so she wrote him a letter. Unfortunately, it arrived on Monday instead of Saturday. All this time he had been in agony, thinking she didn't want to see him on Saturday—or ever again. Instead, she had a family commitment.

The note went on to tell him briefly about her week. She said she hoped he liked his gift, which he did. He had to admit he hadn't been able to touch the Bible since Saturday afternoon, but he would get right back to it. She said she would try to visit again soon. She also told him that she was praying for him every day. Before she signed off, she had written, *"Goodbye for now, my prince."*

She had signed her name at the bottom of the page in larger handwriting. If he had read the sentence above her signature when he first looked at the note, he could have spared himself some grief. He smiled to himself. Then he felt like shouting. Actually, if he could have, he would have loved to jump high in the air—or better yet, into a pool. He wished he was at home, where he could dive into the pool and swim a million laps.

The next Saturday, just as Monica and Ben were leaving, Hannah arrived to visit Brent. They did not recognize her until she said hello to them on her way in, using a cane with her new walking boot. They watched from the door as their son's face lit up like a Christmas tree when Hannah approached the table. He rushed around to pull out the chair for her to sit down.

Monica looked at Ben, then took his hand. They walked back to the car together, silent but happy, with tears in their eyes. They had been so pleased with their conversation with Brent. He was attending all his AA meetings, and his lawyer had gotten an update from the jail administrator saying that he was a "model resident." And now seeing Hannah visit, and their son's obvious delight, they felt hopeful—that maybe their son would be okay after all.

Chapter Eighteen

Buck sidled into the wooden bench in the courtroom. He was very pleased that his pain was finally beginning to subside, although he still wasn't one hundred percent. He gingerly slid along the slick, thickly varnished surface, making room for Nancy to sit next to him. He had just recently moved back into his own bed, much to the relief of both him and Nancy. His arm was mending well, according to the doctor. He never really felt any pain from that injury. The discomfort from his ribs had been so intense that he barely noticed his arm. He would rate his pain at a "three" today, which put him in good spirits. Now, the trick would be to see if he still felt that way after the court proceeding. That would depend on its outcome.

Darius sat and listened quietly, dressed in his Sunday best. He was barely recognizable to those who knew him. In six weeks time, he had made major strides. He was a hard worker and had diligently done his chores without complaint after Buck's injury. The foreman of Buck's ranch crew had written a letter of reference for him that his lawyer would be presenting on his behalf.

Darius had been very quiet the past three weeks, so much so

that Buck and Nancy really didn't know what he would say if the judge gave him the option of staying on at their home.

The judge listened as the letter about Darius was read, then asked Buck and Nancy about their feelings. They both said that Darius had come a long way, was a helpful member of their household, and that he could stay as long as he would like. Then the judge asked Darius if he would like to continue to work off the remainder of his sentence at the ranch.

Darius stood up and said, "Yes, sir." The judge looked surprised by his answer and his respectful tone of voice.

The judge thought a moment, then spoke. "I hereby render this decision—that Darius be remanded..." He paused a moment, which made everyone take a huge breath. "Be remanded to the custody of Buck and Nancy Davis for the remainder of the summer months. He will continue to work on the ranch as his host family sees fit until the end of August, or if he chooses to continue his education, until the beginning of the school semester, whichever comes first."

Everyone expelled their collective breath at the end of his sentence. Buck and Nancy had huge smiles on their faces as they stood and shook hands with the public defender.

Darius was still quiet and looked down at the floor.

"Aren't you okay with this, Darius?" Nancy asked him.

"I am..."

She could tell something was bothering him. "But?"

"I don't want to go back..." He couldn't finish his sentence.

Buck looked at the judge, who was still standing and speaking to a bailiff.

"Judge?" Buck asked loudly. "Does Darius have to return to the same school in the fall?"

The judge turned his attention to Buck, and thought a moment. "After August, he is free to live, or go to school, wherever he so chooses," the judge said.

Darius still looked sad. Then Buck said, "Last I knew, they have a real nice high school in the town closest to our ranch."

Darius looked up then with watery eyes and tried to smile.

"Let's go home," Nancy said, taking Darius' arm.

"Sounds like a plan, darlin'," Buck said, slowly turning and grabbing his hat from the wooden bench behind him.

Carson stood in the main living area of his modest (by the area's standards) two-bedroom home in Santa Monica. He looked around nervously, making sure everything was just right. He must have adjusted the table setting one hundred times already on the small dinner table. There were new white tapers in new candleholders. Carson was not used to entertaining guests.

He was making some of his family favorites tonight. His parents had a "mixed marriage," as his mother used to put it—German on his mother's side, Norwegian on his father's. He was making Norwegian fish cakes, had ordered lefse online from a company in Wisconsin that Jillian had told him about, and was steaming some fresh vegetables—his California contribution to the meal. He had made his mother's spaetzle as another side, and his grandma's apple kuchen for dessert. He hadn't had many of these foods in years.

The doorbell rang, and he rushed to open it. Luz had a way of taking Carson's breath away every time he saw her, and this time was no different. He regained his composure and invited her in. She handed him a small package containing some dark and milk chocolates from *Cacaosuyo*, an award-winning chocolate manufacturer in Peru.

"You didn't have to do that, Luz, but thank you," he said.

"I know I didn't have to, but I wanted to give you something sweet, because you are so sweet to me," she answered, flashing her dark eyes at him.

He felt like his knees might buckle at any moment. He wanted to take her in his arms and kiss her the way he had that day on the set. But after hearing all her horror stories of her past with men, he didn't want to add himself to the list of those who mistreated her—if he wasn't already on it for his prior poor behavior. Then again, she had called him "sweet." He wasn't sure anyone had *ever* called him that before.

Carson gave her a brief tour of the house. It did have a very nice view. Even though it was not right on the water, it was on a hillside, so one could see the beach and ocean. A wide deck afforded a perfect place to watch the sun set, and Carson hoped they would be done eating in time to watch it go down.

He was the perfect host. Luz was impressed that he had made the dinner. She loved all the foods, her favorite being the apple dessert. She also remarked that no man had ever cooked for her before—other than a professional chef in a restaurant.

"I wanted you to have a taste of my home territory, as you did for me. There aren't any restaurants that have this unique mix of foods, so I decided that I'd better fix them myself," he said, relieved that she had enjoyed the food.

After they finished, they walked out onto the deck. The sea air smelled fresh, and their timing was perfect to watch the setting sun. As they neared the railing, Luz took Carson's hand, and his heart leapt. They had been seeing each other every few days over the past couple of weeks. He could have spent every free moment with her, but he didn't want to scare her away.

The movie was just wrapping up. They would have been done sooner, but bad weather at Yosemite had caused a slight delay. Carson did not want the filming to end. Actually, neither of them wanted that, but didn't want to say so to the other. Instead, they kept their thoughts to themselves.

"So," Carson finally said after his heart slowed down to a more normal rate. He was almost afraid to ask, but he had to find out. "What are your plans when we are done in a few days?"

"I have my condo and rental car for another ten days. Then... I will return to Lima," she said.

Carson's heart and countenance sank faster than the setting sun. He had known that it was too good to be true. Someone like Luz belonged with someone—well, someone he would never be.

"Oh," he replied weakly, looking down. He couldn't come up with any other words. His disappointment was weighing on his heart like a heavy anchor.

"Aren't you going to ask me why?" she asked him softly.

"Not really. I'm pretty sure I know why. I understand," he said.

"You do?"

"I do. You need to go on with your life, and you don't need someone..."

"That's not why," she said.

"It isn't? Then, why, Luz?" he asked, his heart breaking.

"I'm going back to Lima to get married in my home church," she said, "with my family present."

He had thought his heart was breaking before; now it was disintegrating.

"You're getting married?" he asked, his words sounding almost like a statement or an accusation.

"I am hoping so. It depends," she said.

"On what?" he asked, starting to feel angry. It had been such a special evening. She even liked the lefse and his apple kuchen. Now she was saying that she would be leaving and getting married.

"On whether or not you will come home with me—and marry me," she said.

Carson wasn't certain about what he just heard. "What?"

"I am asking you—if you would marry me, Carson," she said.

Carson felt dizzy and had to grab the railing on the deck.

"Are you okay, *mi novio*?" she asked, concerned as she put her hand on his free arm.

"Yes—and yes! I'm okay—and I would be honored to marry you, Luz. I am in love with you," he said.

"And I am in love with you, too, Carson Stone," Luz replied, then kissed him from the depth of her being.

Chapter Nineteen

Rick tied his own tie on his special day. He had been practicing every morning with Robert for the last month, the two of them standing side by side in front of the huge mirror above the double sinks in Robert and Karen's bathroom.

Rick was very proud that he had caught on so quickly, and now he had it down to a science. Robert remarked that Rick was better at it in a month than he was in almost thirty years of practice. The two had matching white shirts and ties for the occasion, and Rick had also been fitted for his first suit, a black, single-breasted affair, that accentuated his dark hair and eyes.

Rick had used some styling gel and his hair was pulled away from his face, making him look more mature than his ten years. He used his comb and touched it up one last time. He wanted everything to be perfect on this day.

Rick and Robert put on their suit coats almost simultaneously, then met Karen, who was anxiously waiting for them at the bottom of the stairs. She caught her breath at the first glimpse of them together, her husband and her soon-to-be son, the two men she loved and adored.

She could feel the pressure behind her eyes, and had to work very hard not to cry. To keep herself from starting to blubber, she pulled her phone out of her purse and told them to stop when they reached the bottom step.

"Let me take a picture of you two handsome men," she said.

Rick beamed when she referred to him as a man, and his mouth spread into a giant smile. Robert put his arm around Rick's shoulder. He remembered back to the first time he had tried to do that. Rick had pulled away, most likely because the only touches he had received in his early years from his late father were slaps, or worse. Now Rick didn't even flinch, but instead enjoyed the feeling of his new papa's embrace.

After a mini-photo shoot, the soon-to-be family hustled into the car and drove to the courthouse. It was a Saturday morning, and the judge was doing them a favor, meeting them and the Romanos in her chambers at ten a.m. She herself had two adopted children, and when she heard the stories behind both adoptions, she decided that she could do them privately and on a weekend. Both families were very grateful.

A catered celebration would ensue at John and Jillian's home at noon. Karen's brother was coming down from Santa Barbara, and Robert's brother was coming up from San Diego. Their next-door neighbors, the Smiths, would be there as well. They had barely spoken a word to these people over the years they had lived next to one another. Mostly they just gave them friendly waves of their hands in passing.

That all changed the day Rick hit a baseball into the Smith's backyard. He had gone to their front door, rung the bell, and politely asked if he could get his baseball, with Robert standing behind him for support. Rick was nervous, thinking they would be angry at him. That was often the response he got for everything in his life from the adults he knew.

Instead, the Smiths invited him and Robert in for some lemonade. Both Smiths were huge Dodger fans, which Karen and Robert would have never guessed. Rick talked about the players with them, and they became instant friends. Karen and Robert invited the couple over that evening for dinner, and they had been getting together on a regular basis ever since.

Before Rick came to live with them, Robert and Karen had never realized the ways a child could open doors previously unopened. They met a nice couple at a parent-teacher conference, whose son was in a couple of Rick's classes, and they were also getting to know the parents of the other children on Rick's summer baseball team. Their social network was growing by leaps and bounds. Their entire lives were beginning to change—in such new and wonderful ways.

John, Jillian, Marty, and Michael were waiting for them when they arrived at the courthouse. There were huge smiles all around, and Michael took photos of the new families. Karen remarked that he would make a great photographer, as he grouped them in many different poses on the steps, then by the courthouse sign. He took groups shots, individual shots, twosomes, entire families, and both families together. At the end, John insisted that Michael get in at least one of the photos, and he finally acquiesced.

Once in the chambers, Rick went first, being declared Ricardo Robert Wilson. His birth certificate had no middle name on it, so he had asked if he could have Robert for a middle name, which had made Robert cry for the first time in his adult life.

Then it was Marty's turn. She became Marty Jo Johnson Romano, and she beamed as she and John hugged. Marty finally had a father. John finally had a daughter.

Tears were flowing freely at the end of the proceedings, including the judge's. Karen told Jillian that she never thought she would be a mother. She had prayed and prayed to be one, and now she was. She decided that it had all been worth the wait.

Back at the Storybook-style house, the caterers were all set up and ready. There was a huge cake with both Rick and Marty's new names on it, along with tacos and other Mexican specialties from Paco's Tacos. It was Rick's favorite food, other than pancakes.

John and Jillian had invited all of their friends. Pete and Kelly were showing off the twins' latest "tricks," as Pete called them. Gus was a fast crawler and was also starting to pull himself up. Grace was trying to crawl, and would rock back and forth on her hands and knees. She loved to roll over and over and over to get places in the meantime.

Kelly was doing the books for both of Pete's gyms, and they were starting to talk about the possibility of a third. If that happened, they would have to hire another businessperson to help. Pete was never so happy or proud in his life, with his beautiful family doing well, and his health clubs a huge success.

Buck, Nancy, and Darius walked in together. Buck was much improved, and was beginning to do light chores again. He said Darius had been a great help, and would be sorely missed during the day when he started his final semester of high school in the fall—in their town—he announced with a big smile. He also cornered John privately, telling him he wanted more information one of these days about that "adult adoption stuff," as Buck put it.

Alan and Bev, Carol and Jerry arrived together, along with a sweet little girl about Rick's age named Angela. They said that they had been inspired by all these people adopting or doing other good things for young people, and had signed up to be "foster grandparents." Angela was their first "grandchild," and Carol was glowing. She had always hoped that her children would have children, but it still hadn't happened and they were both in their mid-thirties, and Jerry and his late wife had been childless. They and Angela had only been matched recently, and had only met with her a few times, but Carol said it felt like it was a match made in heaven. John and Jillian nodded with understanding and appreciation of that sentiment.

Greta and Drew arrived, and Jillian could see immediately that things were going better.

"We're hoping to start a family soon," Greta and Drew told Jillian when they had a private moment. Drew put his arm around Greta's shoulders and hugged her close. They looked at each other with such love in their eyes. It was a wonderful sight to behold.

Bobbi and Brooks arrived, newly wed the weekend before, but right back at work at the ever-growing and improving Esperanza Workshop, which they would rename as the Esperanza Center when they eventually reached their programming goals.

More and more people wanted to donate to the project, or help in some way. They had recently hired a volunteer coordinator, and that was very helpful as they continued to expand their services to the community. They also hoped to hire a nurse practitioner to oversee the free healthcare services they were just beginning to dispense on a limited basis. Carol and Jillian had both helped out on occasion, and other doctors and nurses had been volunteering a shift or two per month.

Greta was going to advise them regarding other forms of art that might be taught, and suggested they use college art students as instructors, who could teach and learn from the experience at the same time. Drew suggested seminars be taught about how to manage money wisely on a tight budget, and said he would be willing to teach the first one in the fall. It was a very exciting time, and it seemed the possibilities were endless for the future.

Luz and Carson announced in private their plans to marry in Lima. After the party, they had a private appointment set up with a jeweler to buy their rings. John and Jillian hugged them and told them that if they had time before they left, they hoped they would come to the house for dinner to celebrate.

Marianna and a guest were in attendance. She had been doing great business ever since the Oscars. When Luz heard her speaking about her work, she asked for an appointment with her as soon as possible, or else when she returned to Los Angeles at a later date. Marianna said she would be honored to make a dress for Luz, and would make time for her in the coming week.

Monica and Ben surprised them. Monica had been noncommittal about attending at first, but decided that she and Ben needed friends, and needed to *be friends*, to others. Monica mentioned they were considering selling their mansion. They were tired of the Hollywood scene, and what it had cost them and their family. They were actually considering moving back to Monica's hometown a few hours north of Los Angeles. She had fled it after high school, but now thought perhaps she could build a new aquatic center there and begin a swimming program, with free lessons for those who couldn't afford them and training scholarships for those who excelled in the sport.

They also told John and Jillian the story about Brent visiting Hannah in the hospital, and Hannah visiting Brent in jail. They said they hadn't seen their son smile like that since he was a boy Rick's age. They both teared up as they spoke about their renewed hopes for their family in the future.

If they thought Monica and Ben's appearance was a surprise, it couldn't touch the arrival of the younger Romanos.

"We thought you couldn't come!" John said with tears in his eyes.

"We couldn't miss celebrating the arrival of the newest

Romano," Maria said. Then they all took turns hugging and kissing Marty.

"Also, I needed one last weekend adventure before I begin my new job," Tommy said.

They all looked surprised at that announcement, including John Anthony and Alison.

"Whom are you going to work for?" John asked.

Tommy pulled Maria to his side gently. "It's whom am I going to work *with*. It sounded like working with your wife was a good deal, so I decided to follow your lead, Zio. Meet my new employer—Maria," he said, with that famous Romano grin.

They all hugged again, with congratulations all around. "We'll tell you more about it later. We can stay until tomorrow afternoon," Tommy said, looking more happy and excited than he had in a long time.

It was time to cut and serve the cake. Everyone sang "Happy Adoption Day" to the tune of "Happy Birthday," to Rick and Marty. They each took turns cutting the cake and making a wish, but they both knew that they had already had their biggest wishes come true.

So had John and Jillian. They looked around at all the people they loved. So many friends and family members! It was difficult to remember back to what it had been like two years before.

John shook his head in disbelief. He had never had so many friends and loved ones in all his years. It had taken a good long time to figure out this thing called life, but eventually, through trial and error, and mostly through faith and the grace of God, it all had worked out.

Jillian thought about all the challenges each one of the people present, including herself, had had in the last few months and years. It reminded her of math class back in elementary school, where each student had a pad of "scratch" paper to help them work out the problems. Sometimes there was a lot of erasing and crossing out going on, but in the end, one would usually get the correct answer. She was happy that she, and the people she loved, had finally found their answers.

Jillian turned and smiled at John, who was already looking at her and smiling, and took his hand in hers. Marty walked back over to her mom and dad, and they all hugged each other one more time. It was a day they would never forget. One of many, many, more to come.

That night, after they sent their family members to bed, John and Jillian cleaned up the last of the dishes from a frozen yogurt sundae party that had been the "cherry on top" of a perfect day. They had loved hearing more about Tommy's plans to work with Maria, and also about Marty and Michael's departure plans in a few weeks. Jillian hoped that somehow they might connect with Luz and Carson when they arrived in their new locale.

John and Jillian were tired, but their adrenaline was still running high after such an exciting day. They sat down wearily at the breakfast nook and held hands across the table.

"What a day!" John exclaimed.

"It's always a great day when one becomes a parent," Jillian responded, smiling at him.

Just then they heard a little meow. Lucy, the orange-haired cat, was finally ready to come out of hiding. The place had been filled with people and noise since just after the noon hour. She had quarantined herself to the laundry room once the first guest had arrived. Now that it was just her and her favorite two people left up, she was looking for some loving.

"Hi, honey," Jillian said to Lucy, picking her up from the floor, where the cat was nuzzling her ankles. She stroked the purring fur ball, then rubbed her chin against the silky spot on the top of her head between her ears.

"Lucy," John said. The cat looked at him and purred even louder. He smiled at the two of them, then added quietly, "I'll never forget the first time I saw you holding Lucy."

"Neither will I," Jillian said, looking into his eyes.

"We have a lot to thank Lucy for, don't we?" he asked seriously.

Jillian nodded her head, and looked at her husband lovingly. "Thank God she ran away from you that day, or we may have never met," she said softly.

"Yes, thank God," he agreed, reaching out for her left hand.

He held it and lifted it, looking at the rings on her finger, then into Jillian's eyes. "Look at what you started, Lucy," he said, his eyes never leaving his wife's.

They moved toward one another, and kissed each other gently from across the table, trying not to squish poor Lucy. The cat didn't seem to mind, however, as she purred even louder when their lips met. They realized a moment later that they were in a group hug with their cat, and it made them both laugh.

They parted and smiled at one another.

"I'll love you forever, Jillian."

"I'll love you, forever, John."

Chapter Twenty

EASTER 2046

John put on his dark suit coat and looked in the full-length mirror. Jillian emerged from the walk-in closet in their bedroom suite, stopped, and quietly watched him button his shirt. She was dressed in a dress that had been made for the occasion by their friend, and now famous designer, Marianna. Marianna had salvaged bits and pieces of the dress Jillian had worn on their wedding day, brilliantly working them and new material into another remarkable creation.

"It still fits," John said to his image. Jillian wasn't surprised. John still took walks with her every day, swam often, did yoga, and even did some light weight work—not bad for a ninety-year-old.

"You sound surprised," she said as she came up behind him and slid her arms around his waist, the tie he had worn on their wedding day in her right hand. She hugged him, and he held her arms.

"Well, it has been thirty years, you know," he said, that grin that Jillian loved so much stretching across his face, reflected in the mirror. "How can it possibly be that long, Jillian?" he asked, turning around to face her.

"I don't know," she said truthfully. "It feels like it was yesterday that we said 'I do.'"

"It was the best day of my life when I married you. That day, and every day since."

It never ceased to amaze Jillian how this man could make her love him more each passing day for the past thirty years. She smiled at him and then kissed his cheek.

"Same here," she said softly, putting her hands on his chest, one touching the crisp, white shirt he was wearing for the first time, the other the soft material of the ancient jacket. She looked him in the eyes. "Should I do your tie, or will you?" She knew he had some arthritis in his hands and it was difficult for him to tie it, but she still liked to ask out of respect.

"Why don't you do it this time? It's a special occasion, and I want it to be just right," he answered.

It was thirty years ago on Easter Sunday, at five p.m., that the two stood at the altar at Grace Lutheran Church and said their vows before Pastor Jim. In just an hour, they were going to renew those vows at five p.m.—again, with Pastor Jim officiating. Their actual anniversary date was still two days away, but they had wanted to do this when their family could be present.

Tommy and Maria, John Anthony and his wife and two sons, Tommy John and Anthony, had flown in early on Saturday. Alison, her husband, and daughter had arrived on Friday night. Marty and her husband, Michael, were also home from their medical mission work in South America. Their grown children, John Martin and Judy Jo, flew in from their home cities, where John worked as a surgeon and Judy was still in medical school.

Everyone was going to Leo's for dinner after the ceremony. Leo was no longer with them on this earth, unfortunately, but Leonardo, Danielo, Adelina, and their children still owned and operated the restaurant, and still made the best Italian food around. They had also remained great friends throughout the years, the sons even teaching Italian cooking classes at the original Esperanza Center. The L.A. Center was now just one of many such Centers in the nation, and one of a myriad of philanthropic projects of the John and Jillian Johnson Romano Foundation.

This time, Karen, Robert, and Rick, who now liked to be called by his given name, Ricardo, would be in attendance at their ceremony. Ricardo was now the director of the Esperanza Center in Los Angeles. Pete and Kelly, who had just celebrated their thirtieth anniversary as well, along with the twins, who were both recently engaged—they seemed to do everything in tandem—would be joining them.

Drew and Greta, and their daughter, who was home from her art studies in Europe, would be in attendance as well. Carol and Jerry were coming from their home not far away. Luz, and Luz' and Carson's daughter, Sol, and son, Carson, Jr., would be there, too.

Nancy's grandson was coming to take photographs again. Darius, his wife, Keisha, and sons Buck and "DJ," a nickname for Darius Jack, were on their way. Darius, whom Buck and Nancy legally adopted, and his family now lived in the ranch house, and ran the ranch. They continued a program through the Esperanza Center for at-risk youth that had been instituted a few years after Darius came to live with them. A number of young people had lived at the ranch over the years, receiving another chance. It was one of the most successful programs the Center offered.

Nancy and Buck, both in their late nineties, were residents at the nursing home where Jillian had once worked briefly, and where she had volunteered for years afterward. John and Jillian were going to visit them the next day to take them some tiramisu and show them photos of the renewal ceremony and all the people in attendance.

Monica and Ben, Bart, Brent and his wife, Hannah, and son, Luke, would also be there. With so many loved ones gathered together in one place, their service was sure to be a very special and blessed event.

John, Jillian, and Pastor Jim had recreated their original wedding ceremony as closely as possible. Pastor Jim read their scripture verse, Second Corinthians, chapter five, verse seventeen, once again, and remarked how it had set the tone for their marriage. He mentioned that thirty years later, its message still rang true in their relationship, and would until the very end of their life's journey together.

As John and Jillian faced one another and renewed their vows, their eyes never left the other's, and it felt like they were the only two people on earth. Jillian called moments like that their own version of a "mind meld," where they didn't even have to speak to convey their innermost thoughts.

The happy couple kissed at the end of the ceremony, which still made Jillian feel weak in the knees. She was sure that few people were ever as blessed as her and John. She was still in love with her husband, and she knew that he was still in love with her, too. They also had another kind of love now, the kind that comes from thirty years of the ups and downs of life. *But mostly ups,* Jillian thought to herself.

John's acting career had been active until just a few years ago. He had recently done a commercial for a children's hospital, but that was a rarity. He had become one of the most beloved and honored actors, and later directors, of his era, winning Oscars in several categories. His biography had been published just as he officially retired, around the same time as Jillian's novel based on their own story had been published and well-received. Recently she had been approached about writing it into a screenplay.

John still made personal appearances at acting classes from time to time at the various Esperanza Centers, especially the original one in Los Angeles, and still inspired and encouraged many young actors and directors to use their gifts for the good of others.

Jillian and John had worked on a number of film projects together over the years, due to the insight of the late Academy Award-winning director Carson Stone, who gave Jillian her first taste of screenwriting and directing. One of her greatest joys was writing a movie that starred her husband in the lead male role. Carson's wife, Luz, played the female lead opposite John, as she had many years before, and Carson directed. They *all* won "Oscars" for it, something Jillian would never have dreamed when she set out for California to become a writer thirty-one years before.

The celebratory dinner at Leo's was exceptional, as always, and the restaurant was filled with the cheerful voices of people John and Jillian loved dearly. As he had before the meal on their wedding night, John said a table prayer that brought tears to Jillian's eyes, and Tommy and Marty made toasts in their honor.

After dinner, John Anthony, Alison, and others all briefly shared something they admired, or had learned, from John and Jillian and their special relationship over the years. These words of love were the best gifts the couple could have ever received. It didn't get much better than that, and John and Jillian were both humbled and honored. The entire evening was both magical and memorable.

That night, as they had been thirty years before, John and Jillian were taken via limousine to the house on the beach where they had spent their wedding night. It had belonged to them for twenty-five years now. John had bought the house from his friend

Kathy J. Jacobson

and had surprised Jillian with it as a "gift" on their fifth anniversary. The beach house was one of their favorite places on earth, a spot where they had shared many special private and family memories over the years.

Two days later, their family and friends now back at their homes, it was officially John and Jillian's thirtieth wedding anniversary date, March the twenty-seventh. They got up early as usual, Jillian attributing that to all of John's early "makeup calls" in the field of acting. They kissed each other and wished each other a happy anniversary, before anything else that morning.

It was a beautiful sunny day, just as it had been thirty years before on their wedding day. John had insisted that he prepare breakfast for this special occasion—just something simple. He decided to recreate the meal he had made—or as he had referred to it that day—had "gathered"—for Jillian the morning after she had decided to stay, rather than leave, the house she had now called home for so many years. There were croissants, breads and jams, a fresh fruit and cheese plate, fresh-squeezed orange juice, and coffee. It was a perfect meal, and brought back fond memories.

They ate together in the breakfast nook, and talked about the past weekend—the renewal of vows ceremony, and about all that was going on in the lives of their family and friends. They were so proud of the many wonderful things their family members were doing—not only in their professional work, but their generous and giving ways.

They couldn't help but remember, as they ate this special breakfast, how thankful they were to God that John came back to the house the day Jillian had planned to leave. He had come back only minutes before a taxi pulled up to take her away—forever. They smiled as they thought of the notes John had written, asking her to stay, because he thought he was the *right person* for her. She had accepted his invitation to stay—as it turned out —permanently.

"That was a good day," John said, taking Jillian's hand in his, then kissing it.

"Yes, it was," Jillian agreed, looking at John with so much love in her eyes. They toasted to one another with their orange juice, and thoroughly enjoyed the simple, yet meaningful fare.

"I'll clean up this time, John," Jillian said when they had finished, recalling that he had done so on that day long ago. He looked a bit tired to her that morning, but it had been quite a full weekend, so that was to be expected. She felt a bit worn out herself after all the church services leading up to Easter, a house full of company, not to mention their special event.

Jillian and John stood up from the table. "Okay, if you insist, but just one more thing," he said, moving toward her. He put his arms around her and pulled her close. "I'll love you forever, Mrs. Romano," he said. They had said these words—I'll love you forever—to each other each night, ever since the eve of their marriage.

"I'll love you forever, Mr. Romano," she replied. They kissed and held each other for a long moment.

"I'm going to the library to read," John said, a look of happy contentment on his face.

"I'll join you soon," she answered, and began to clear the table, smiling out of sheer joy.

Jillian put the juice and jams away, unplugged the coffee pot, and then put the dishes into the sink. As she did, she looked up and noticed John walking back into the room, coming her way. She wiped her hands on a towel and turned toward him.

"Did you change your mind, sweetheart?" she asked.

John didn't answer her, but just stood there, a strange look on his face. She had seen that look before—a long time ago. Fear shot through her body as she moved toward him. The scene seemed to play out in slow motion to her, and she saw it over and over again in her mind for the rest of her life, as she watched John crumble to the floor.

Jillian instinctively knew that this time—he was gone.

Hours later, Jillian came into the kitchen from the garage and put her keys down on the counter. The dishes still sat in the sink, and a package of opened bread was still on the counter. She walked over to the breakfast nook, where she and John had shared so many meals together, including their final one only hours before, and slowly sat down on the bench. She felt like she had aged twenty years since the beginning of the day.

Tommy was in the process of booking his flight back to Los Angeles from Chicago. It reminded Jillian of how he had come to help the first time John had had a major health issue, only months before their marriage. Marty and Carol would arrive the next morning. Carol had offered to come right away, but Jillian had told her to wait. Marty, Tommy, and Carol would go with Jillian the next afternoon to help make "arrangements."

Jillian had known that this day would someday come, or at least thought chances were that John would precede her in death, given their difference in age. She sometimes selfishly hoped that it would end up the other way around, but she knew that John was terrified of living without her. She also knew that he never wanted to live as an invalid, so she guessed that this was the way he would have wanted it to go.

Jillian was deep in thought, and still in shock, and jumped when the doorbell sounded. They had begun leaving the gate open to the driveway the past few years, as the paparazzi had younger stars to hound these days. She wondered who it could be. It was too early for her family or friends.

She walked into the foyer, standing on the black and white marbled floor where she had first been embraced by John, and opened the door. There stood a deliveryman, practically hidden behind a huge glass vase full of yellow roses, just like the ones that had been at the beach house on their wedding night.

"Delivery for Jillian Johnson Romano," the young man announced.

"That's me," she said.

"Thank goodness. I was here earlier—twice—but no one was home."

"I appreciate your persistence," she said kindly, and instructed the young man to set the flowers down on a table. Jillian went back to the kitchen to get some money to tip him. When she returned, she handed him a very large bill and thanked him again. His eyes lit up when he saw the large tip, then asked if she was certain she meant to give him that much.

"Yes, I am certain."

He thanked her profusely and stepped back to his truck lightheartedly.

Jillian walked slowly over to the flowers. The arrangement and vase were exact duplicates of the original from thirty years ago, although instead of two dozen roses, there were thirty of them in the vase. She turned the vase and there was a clear plastic stake, holding a yellow self-stick note. She gently slipped it off the stake and looked at it, holding it like it was the most precious thing in the world.

Written in John's own handwriting, a little shakier than it had been thirty years ago, but still penned in his distinctive style, were the same words he had written on the note on the wedding night bouquet.

Jillian, I'll love you forever. John

Her eyes filled with tears—mostly happy ones. She thought about all the wonderful years she had shared with this man, and how long she had waited for someone like John to come along. It had all been worth the wait for God to send the right person into her life, giving her the gift of many years filled with love and happiness. Now, she would just have to be patient once more, and wait until she could see him again one day—in heaven.

She held up the note again, and read the words one more time. She heard John's voice in her ears, and felt his love in her heart. Then Jillian looked up and said out loud,

"NOTED!"

The End

Questions for Discussion

1. For the second time, the choice for John's female acting co-star is shocking to Jillian. How would you have felt in this situation?

2. Have you ever met someone who seemed "flawless" to you, especially in comparison to yourself? Discuss.

3. As children grow older and move on with new ventures and their own lives, one's household dynamics often change. Have you experienced this? How did you feel? How did you deal with these changes?

4. Tommy has been faithful to Maria the entirety of their relationship, which began on the night of their senior prom. Suddenly, amidst the changes and challenges on the home front, he finds himself being flattered and pursued by an attractive woman, opening up new temptations in his life. How do you think he handled them? What might he have done differently?

5. When Maria and Alison are injured in an accident, Tommy feels at fault. What do you think? Have you ever felt responsible for something bad that happened because of something you did, or didn't do?

6. Just when things are looking up for Monica's family, her son, Brent, seriously injures someone while driving intoxicated. Have you ever been hopeful in some area of your life, only to have your "bubble" suddenly burst in another?

7. If you were Jillian, would you be willing to help Monica, a woman who had previously caused her and John pain? Why or why not?

8. Carol is both excited about the future, but grieving the loss of a life she has known for thirty years. This is a common phenomenon in life. How do you handle goodbyes and new starts?

9. Even though Jillian's "Luz predicament" seems minor in comparison to others' problems, Carol mentions it is "best to talk about it, even if it seems minor. You don't want it to turn into something major." Comment on that thought.

10. Robert and Karen are sick with worry when Rick disappears. What was your first thought when that happened? What good may have come out of the situation in the end?

11. When invited to lunch at Monica's house, Jillian gets a sense of the family's home life. They are real people and a real family, yet are rarely treated as such by society. Every aspect of their lives is followed and scrutinized by the paparazzi. Some people quip that that is the "cost of fame." What do you think about that phrase? Would it be worth it to you?

12. Maria's business is doing well, but is not without its "costs," too. What are they? What did you think of the solution? Would you enjoy working with your spouse or a close friend on a daily basis? What might have been other alternatives?

13. Greta hoped to be a parent one day, but was totally unprepared for the news that she was pregnant. Instead of feeling excited and happy, she felt unhappy and resentful. Discuss.

14. When Drew and Greta lose the baby, Greta blames herself. She has difficulty telling Drew, or anyone, about her feelings (both about the baby and the guilt after losing it.) Her inability to share her burdens causes very unhealthy behaviors. How do you think you would have felt, or what would you have done, in a similar situation?

15. Marty has had her heart set on working in Africa since childhood. Therefore, it was tough to take when Michael admitted he preferred to work elsewhere. How would you have felt? Did you like the outcome of this situation?

16. Marty changed her mind after meeting Luz and realizing there are good people everywhere. Has meeting and talking to someone ever changed your mind about a place, person, or personal plan?

17. Carson Stone had the very painful experience of being left at the altar. Even though he is a very successful Hollywood director, he is very personally insecure and feels unattractive. He has been fearful of loving anyone for many years. Luz, on the other hand, is very attractive physically, but has rarely been respected or loved for the talented, intelligent, and kind person she is. She, too, has never found true love. Discuss these situations.

18. Jillian makes a comment to Luz that perhaps a start to changing others' perceptions of her is to stop dressing so provocatively. Luz answers that her agent wants her to dress that way, and Jillian suggests that Luz start looking for a new agent. What do you think?

19. Brent Bastien wants to see the person he hurt. Do you think this is a good idea? Later, when he visits her and reads to her, he is afraid to touch Hannah's Bible. He feels it is a "book by, and for, good people," and that he wasn't one of them. Thankfully, he changes his mind on another visit and reads the story of the "lost son," and experiences God's grace for the first time. Do you remember a time you needed to hear of God's love and forgiveness, and received it?

20. John and Tommy take a road trip to the family cemetery plot in Belvidere. What did you think of John's gestures at his father's and brother's graves? Do you think it was helpful, even though his family members are no longer living? Have you ever had a similar experience?

21. Darius assumes that Buck has lived a charmed life, but is very wrong in that assumption. Have you ever been very wrong about someone like Darius was about Buck?

22. Many people were given chances to begin anew their relationships and paths together in this book—Carson and Luz; John, Marty, and Jillian; Tommy and Maria; Greta and Drew; Karen, Robert, and Rick; Monica's family; Brent and Hannah; Marty and Michael; Buck, Nancy, and Darius. Life is full of twists and turns, beginnings and endings, and changes in plans. What have been some of the most memorable, or most meaningful ones, in your life?

Author's Note/Acknowledgments

One of my professors used to talk about "the privilege of being invited into people's lives." I have been blessed with that privilege countless times, in a multitude of settings and ways. I believe that writing *Scratch Pad*, and the entire *Noted!* series, has been a way for my heart and mind to process the many and varied situations, and people, I have encountered over the years. I have appreciated the opportunity to remember, and hope and pray that these stories might be a source of strength and peace for my readers. I know that this book, and series, has reminded me of how many times in life we all face situations which require a lot of "working out." But I was also reminded once again, that with faith, there is always hope.

As always, a huge thank you to my family—husband, Jeff, daughter, Kirsten, son Spencer and his wife, Emily, son Jens, my cousins Judy and Pam, the Jacobson clan, and my hospice and church families for their ongoing love and support. A special thanks to Cleo Ware for reading the manuscript. I couldn't do this without all of you!

Kathy J. Jacobson

About the Author

Kathy J. Jacobson has worked in various forms of ministry over the past twenty years—from youth and Christian education coordinator, to campus ministry, rural parish ministry to hospice chaplain.

She lives in the beautiful "Driftless Area" of Southwestern Wisconsin with her husband, Jeff. They have three "children"—all "twenty-something." She is an avid traveler, having visited all fifty states, with most memorable trips to the Holy Land, Papua New Guinea, and Tanzania. She loves music, the theater, hiking and the Wisconsin Badgers, but her true passion is writing. *Scratch Pad* is the fourth book in the *Noted!* "faithful fiction" series.

Check out the entire NOTED! series.

"Kathy J. Jacobson has beautifully written a story weaving the characters lives together in *four books* that are gripping, sentimental, meaningful accounts of relationships, and keep the interest of the reader."

Nancy Fulton Young
Psychologist, Marriage and Family Therapist, and Mediator, Madison, WI

Praise for Scratch Pad

"A great read that has it all—suspense, intrigue, love, conflict, joy, despair and much more. Through the incredible highs and awful lows that are life, those close to Jillian and John see a healthy, loving, forgiving, faith-based relationship and begin to see paths to a full, rich life for themselves."

Rev. Steve Kottke
Assistant to the Bishop, SCSW-ELCA, Madison, WI

"Kathy J. Jacobson addresses several social issues that offer deep understanding of a variety of personalities and human conditions.

She sees life through many different lenses and weaves her knowledge of issues, such as marital insecurity, jealousy, life-threatening diseases, drug and alcohol addiction, faith questioning, aging and grieving, into the daily lives of her characters.

The brilliance of this book, that will touch the lives of people from all faiths and backgrounds, is Jacobson's ability to offer wise counsel, with a masterful and insightful blending of her Christian faith and spiritual beliefs; her ability to relate and care for troubled youth, as well as the famous and wealthy; her wisdom as a mother of three adult children whose wings are soaring; and her deeply rooted and loving marriage of almost thirty years."

Nancy Fulton Young
Psychologist, Marriage and Family Therapist, and Mediator, Madison, WI